THE ADVENTURES OF
THE BAILEY SCHOOL KIDS®
VAMPIRES DON'T WEAR POLKA DOTS

A GRAPHIC NOVEL BY PEARL LOW

BASED ON THE NOVEL BY
MARCIA THORNTON JONES & DEBBIE DADEY

graphix

An Imprint of
■ SCHOLASTIC

FOR MY MOM AND BEST FRIEND, THELMA THORNTON
– MARCIA THORNTON JONES

FOR ALEX – DEBBIE DADEY

I DEDICATE THIS BOOK TO THE IMAGINATION WITHIN
ALL OF US; IMAGINATION THAT ALLOWS US TO SEE THE
WORLD WITH CURIOSITY, WONDER, AND AWE – PEARL LOW

Text copyright © 1990, 2021 by Marcia Thornton Jones and Debra S. Dadey
Art copyright © 2021 by Pearl Low

Library of Congress Control Number: 2020941106

ISBN 978-1-338-73660-1 (hardcover)
ISBN 978-1-338-73659-5 (paperback)

10 9 8 7 6 5 4 3 2 1   21 22 23 24 25

Printed in China   62
First edition, August 2021

Edited by Jonah Newman
Book design by Steve Ponzo
Color flatting by Wes Dzioba
Creative Director: Phil Falco
Publisher: David Saylor

THE KIDS AT BAILEY SCHOOL

EDDIE

MELODY

HOWIE

LIZA

CAREY

BEN

CHAPTER 1 A NEW TEACHER

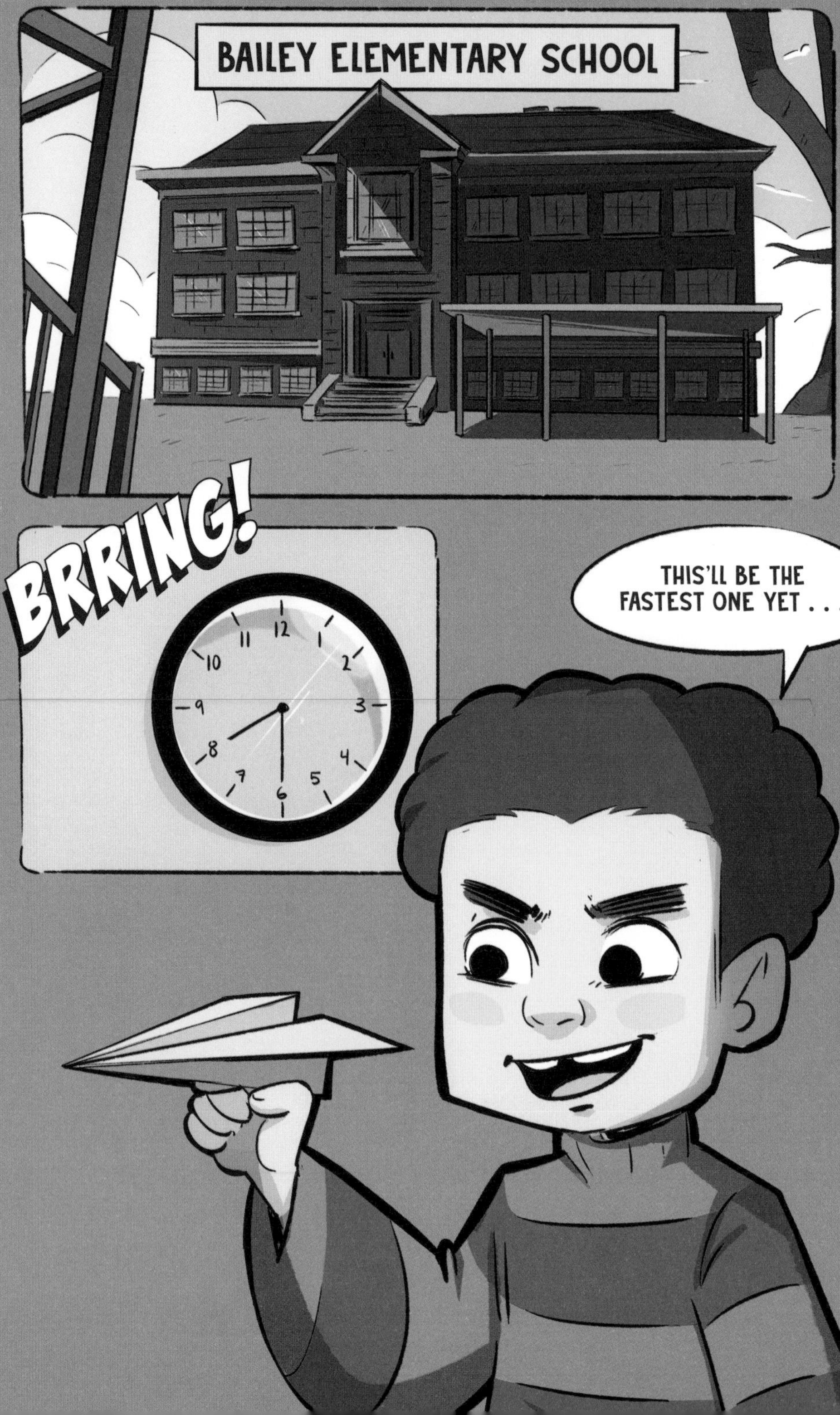
BAILEY ELEMENTARY SCHOOL
BRRING!
THIS'LL BE THE FASTEST ONE YET . . .

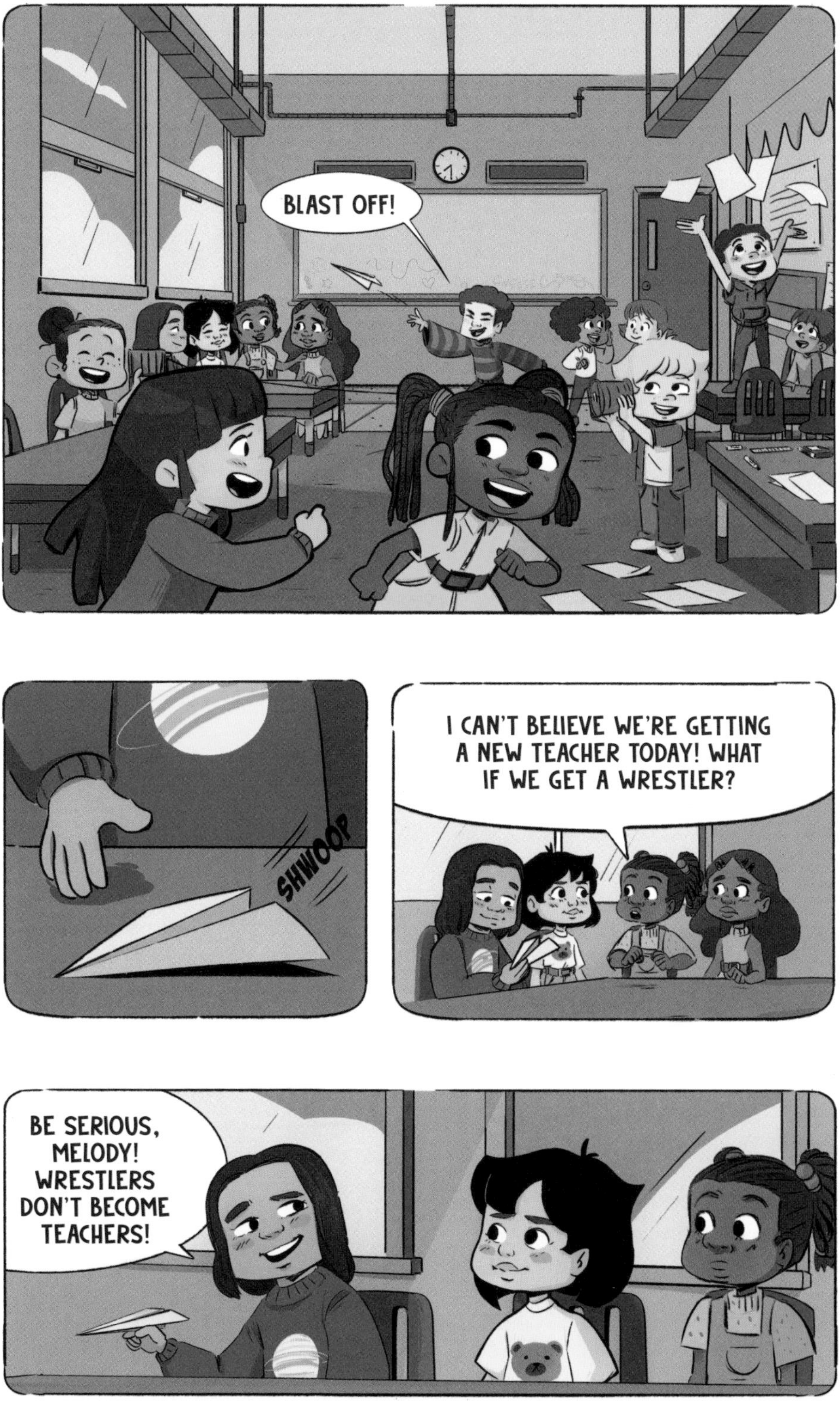
BLAST OFF!
SHWOOP
I CAN'T BELIEVE WE'RE GETTING A NEW TEACHER TODAY! WHAT IF WE GET A WRESTLER?
BE SERIOUS, MELODY! WRESTLERS DON'T BECOME TEACHERS!

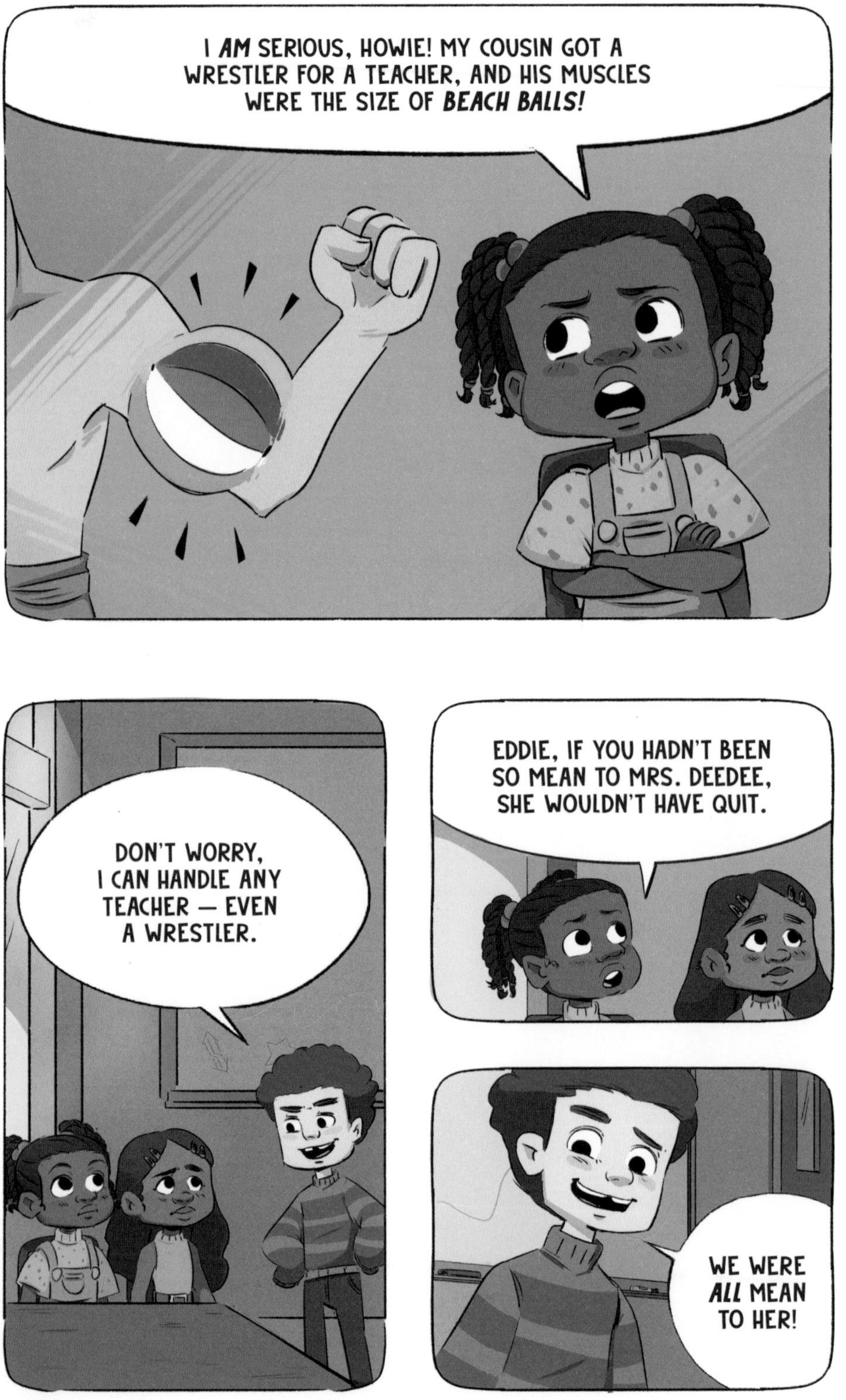
I *AM* SERIOUS, HOWIE! MY COUSIN GOT A WRESTLER FOR A TEACHER, AND HIS MUSCLES WERE THE SIZE OF *BEACH BALLS!*
DON'T WORRY, I CAN HANDLE ANY TEACHER — EVEN A WRESTLER.
EDDIE, IF YOU HADN'T BEEN SO MEAN TO MRS. DEEDEE, SHE WOULDN'T HAVE QUIT.
WE WERE *ALL* MEAN TO HER!

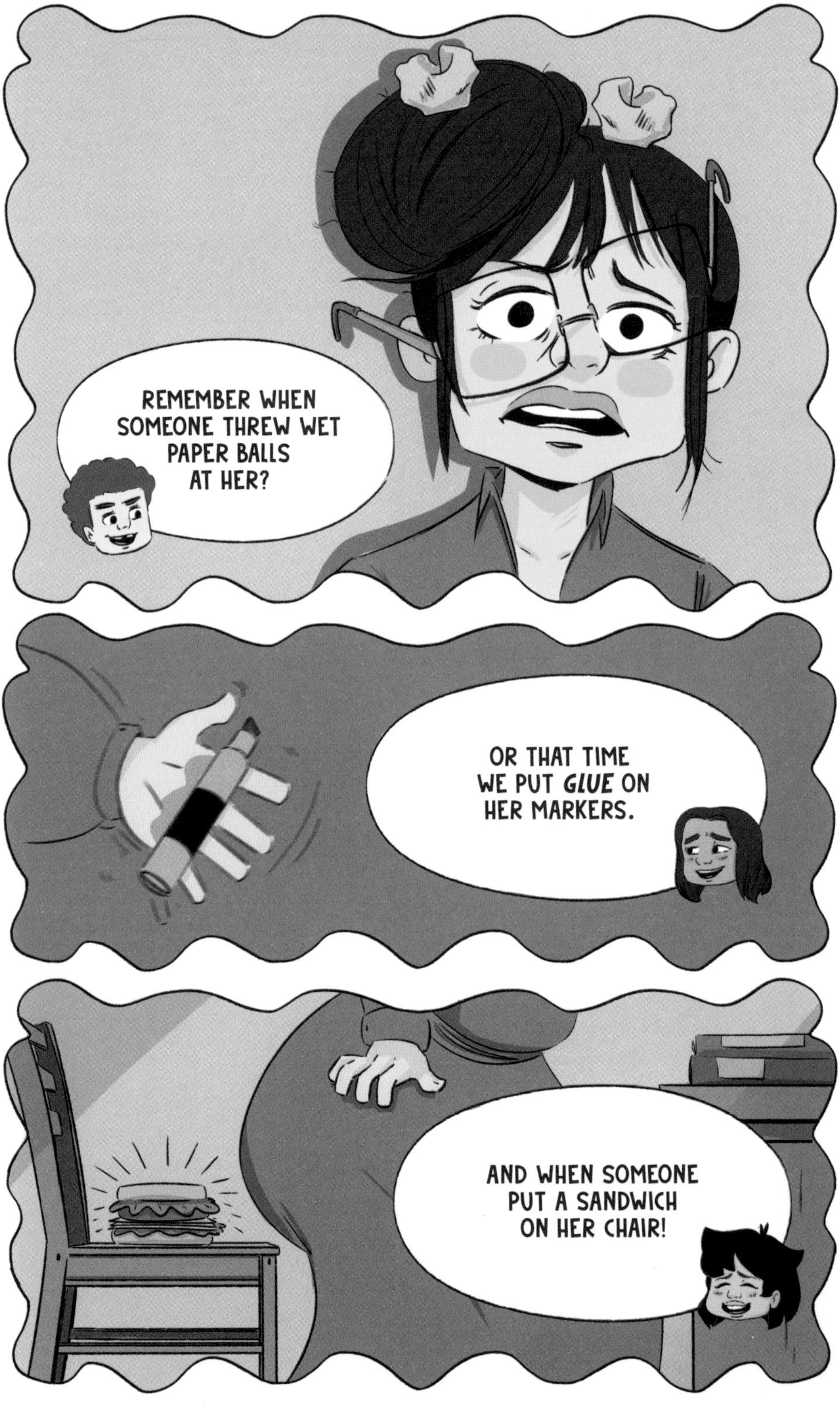
REMEMBER WHEN SOMEONE THREW WET PAPER BALLS AT HER?
OR THAT TIME WE PUT *GLUE* ON HER MARKERS.
AND WHEN SOMEONE PUT A SANDWICH ON HER CHAIR!

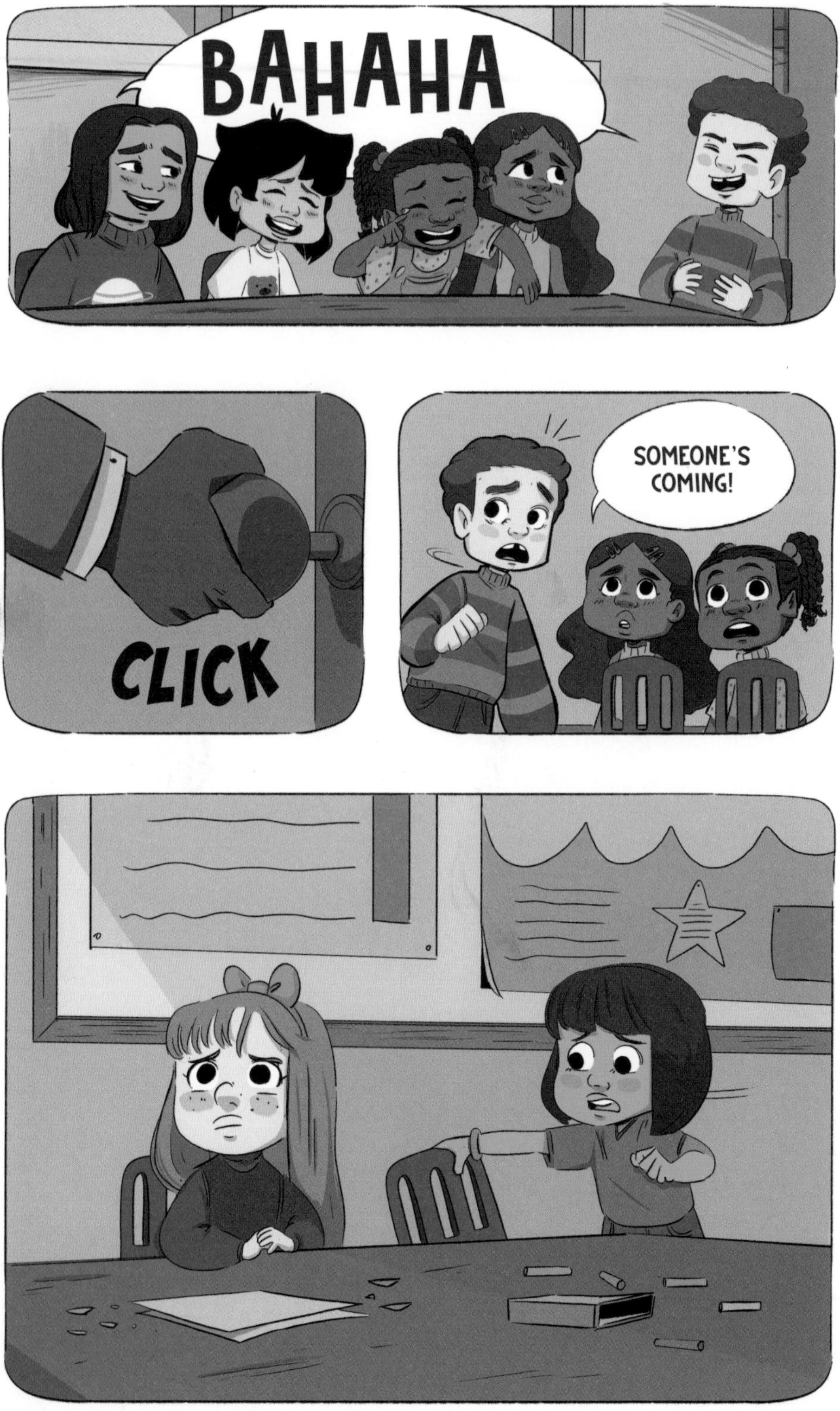
BAHAHA
CLICK
SOMEONE'S COMING!

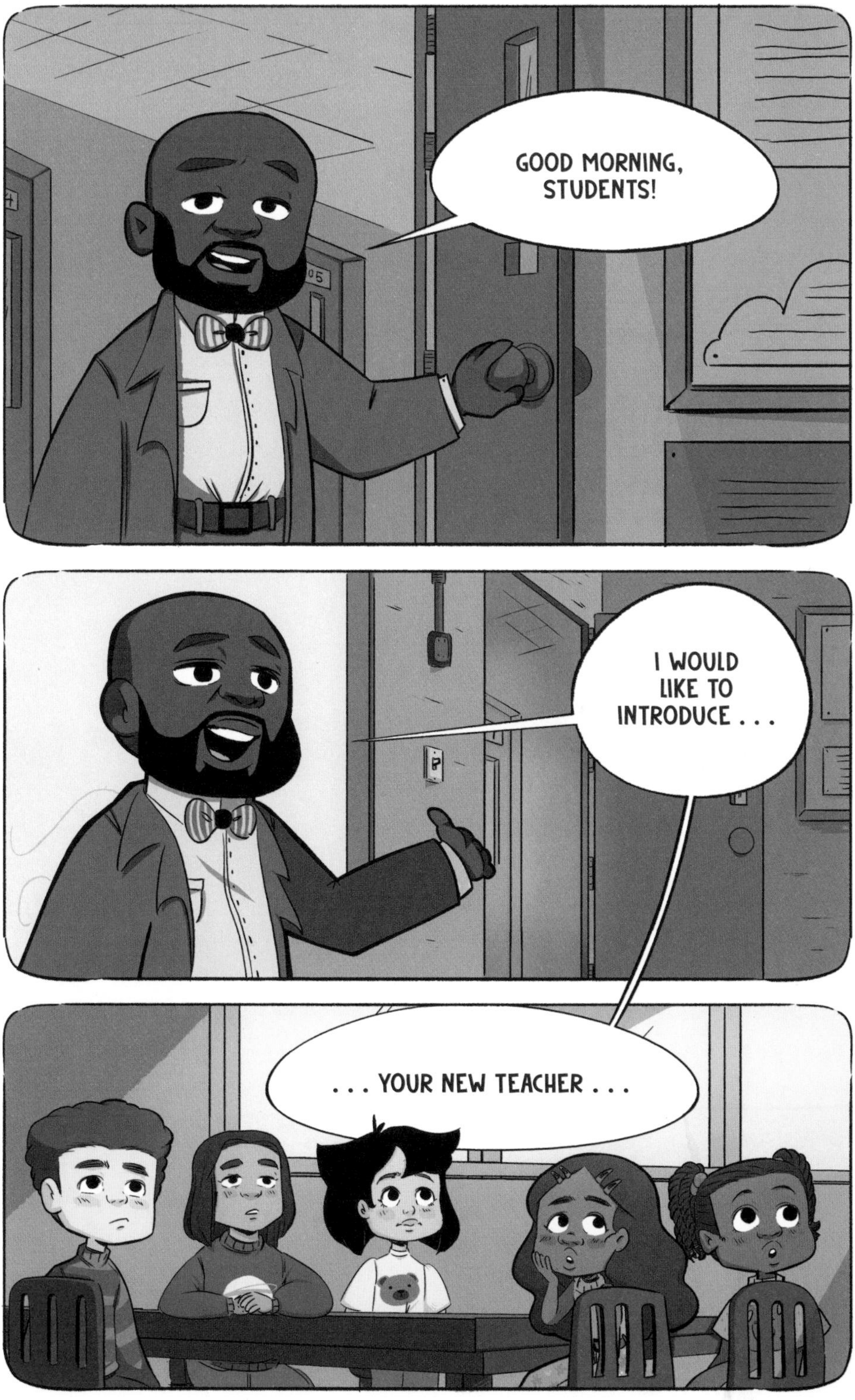
GOOD MORNING, STUDENTS!
I WOULD LIKE TO INTRODUCE . . .
. . . YOUR NEW TEACHER . . .

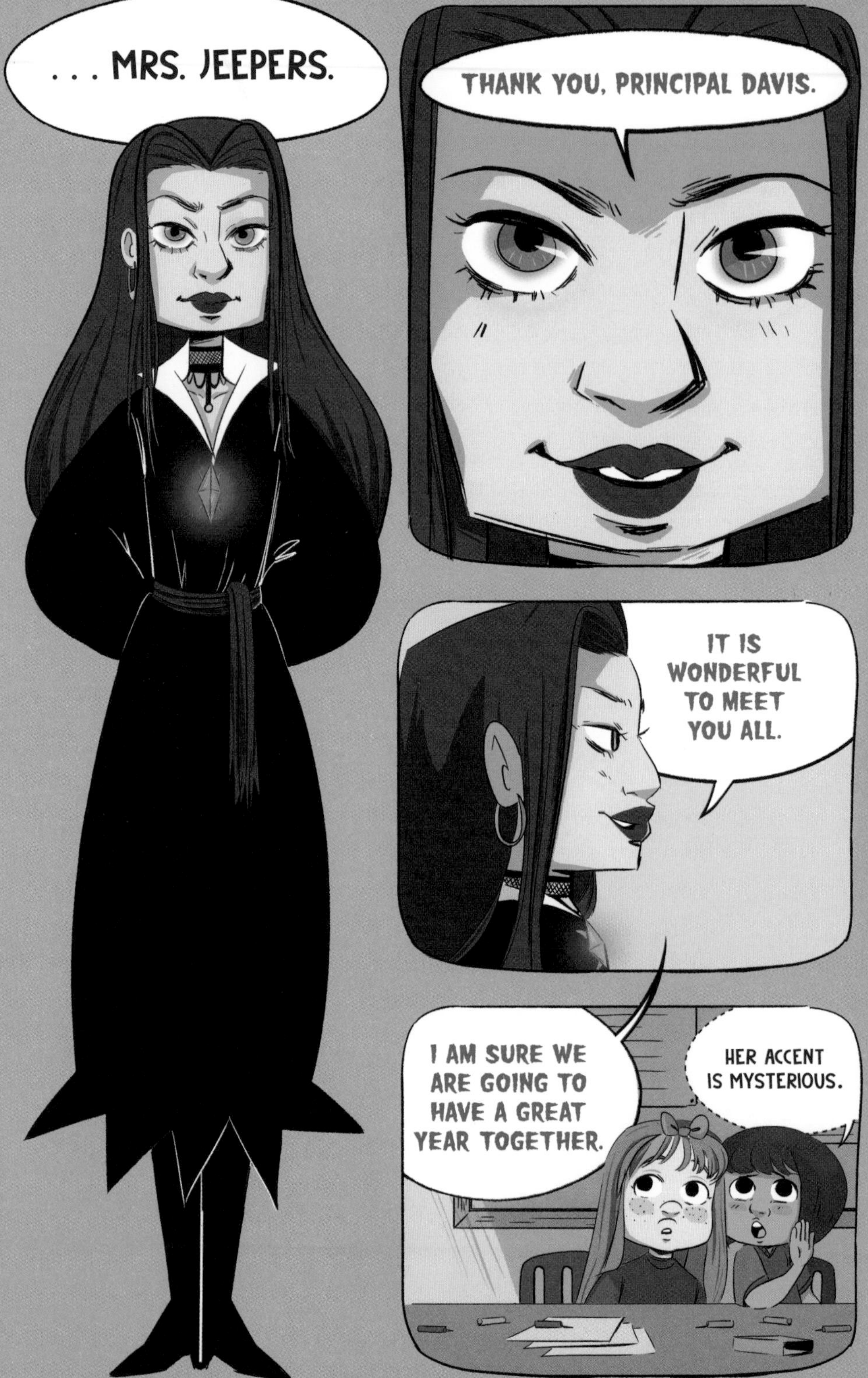
. . . MRS. JEEPERS.
THANK YOU, PRINCIPAL DAVIS.
IT IS WONDERFUL TO MEET YOU ALL.
I AM SURE WE ARE GOING TO HAVE A GREAT YEAR TOGETHER.
HER ACCENT IS MYSTERIOUS.

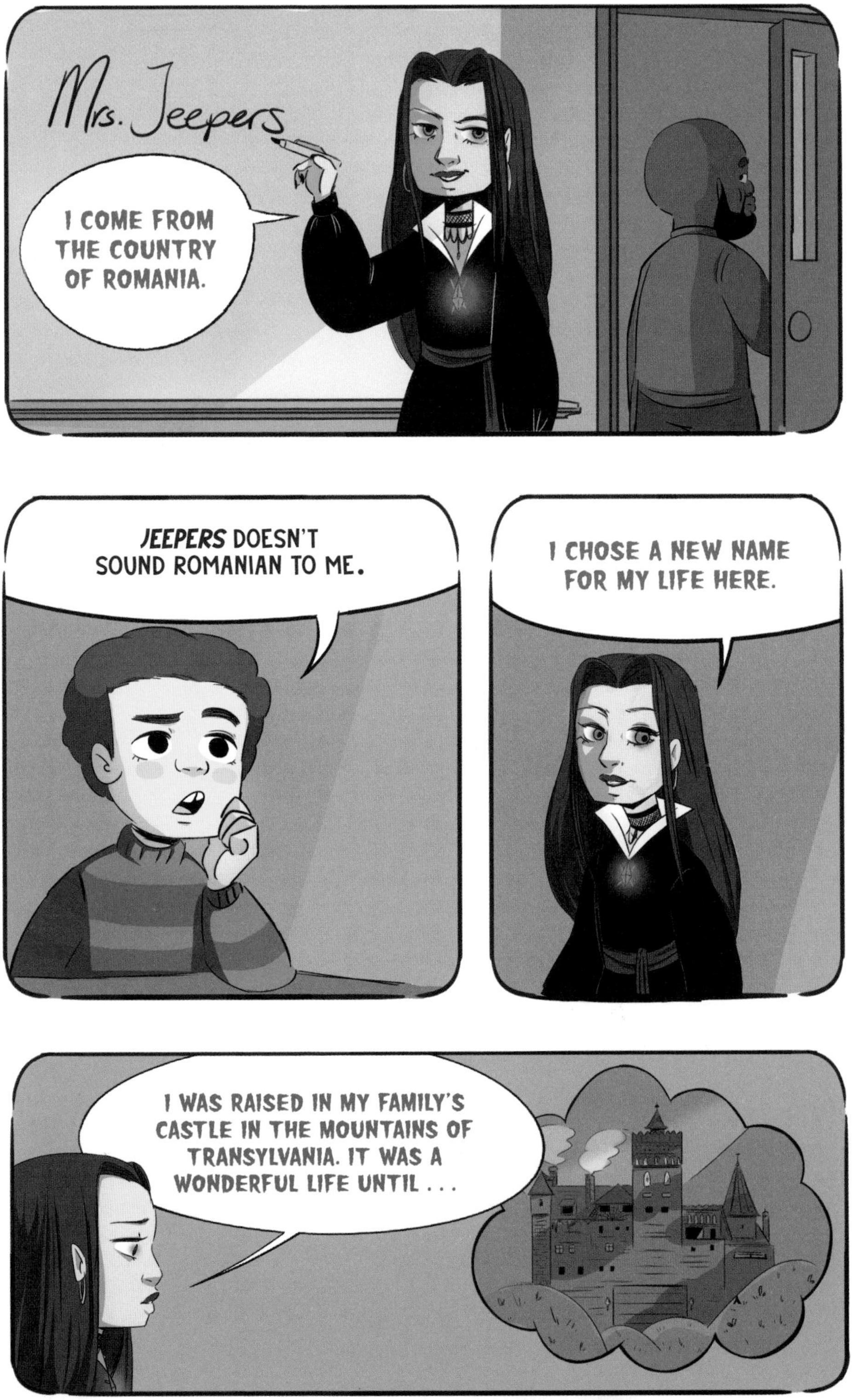
Mrs. Jeepers
I COME FROM THE COUNTRY OF ROMANIA.
JEEPERS DOESN'T SOUND ROMANIAN TO ME.
I CHOSE A NEW NAME FOR MY LIFE HERE.
I WAS RAISED IN MY FAMILY'S CASTLE IN THE MOUNTAINS OF TRANSYLVANIA. IT WAS A WONDERFUL LIFE UNTIL . . .

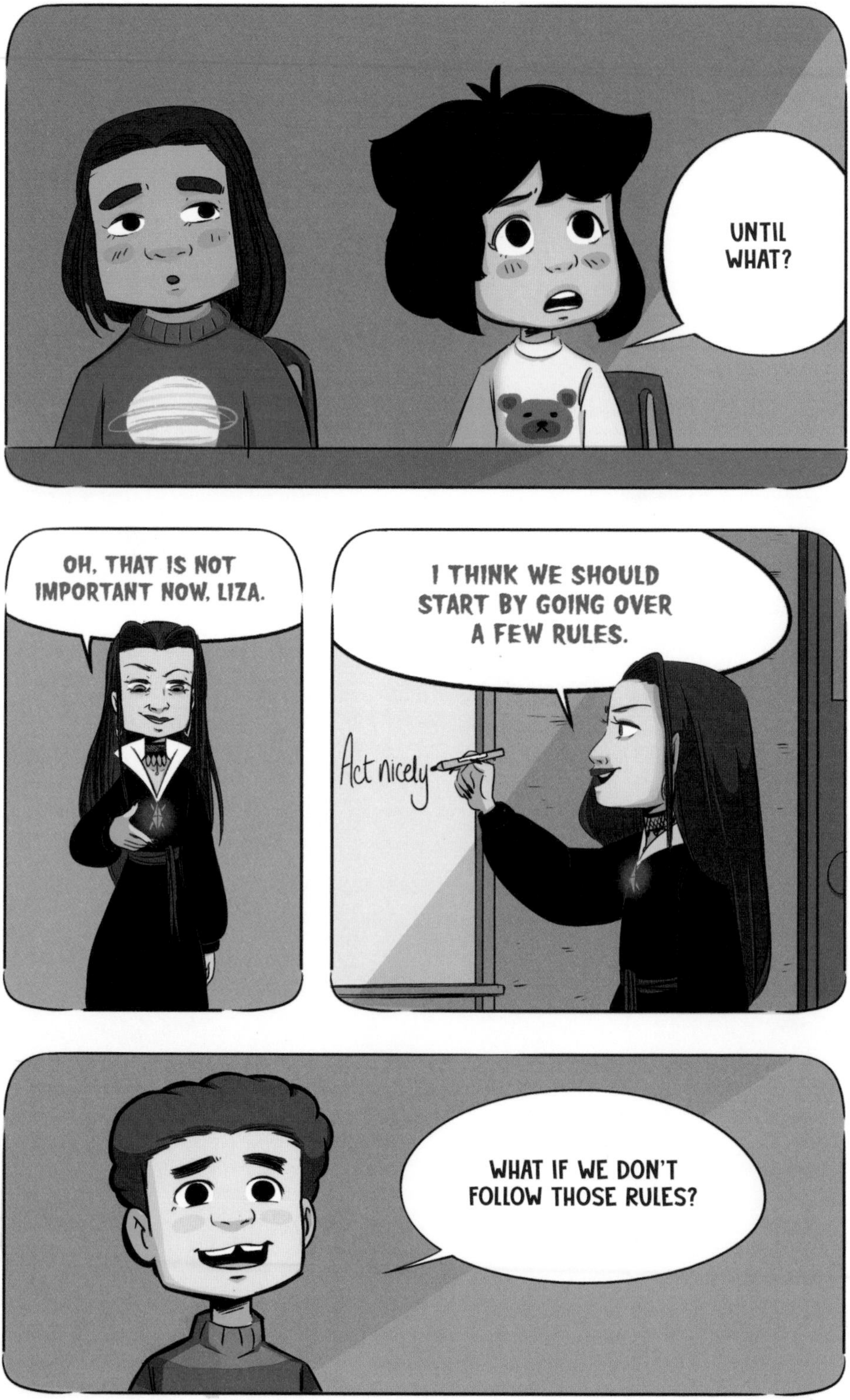
UNTIL WHAT?
OH, THAT IS NOT IMPORTANT NOW, LIZA.
I THINK WE SHOULD START BY GOING OVER A FEW RULES.
Act nicely
WHAT IF WE DON'T FOLLOW THOSE RULES?

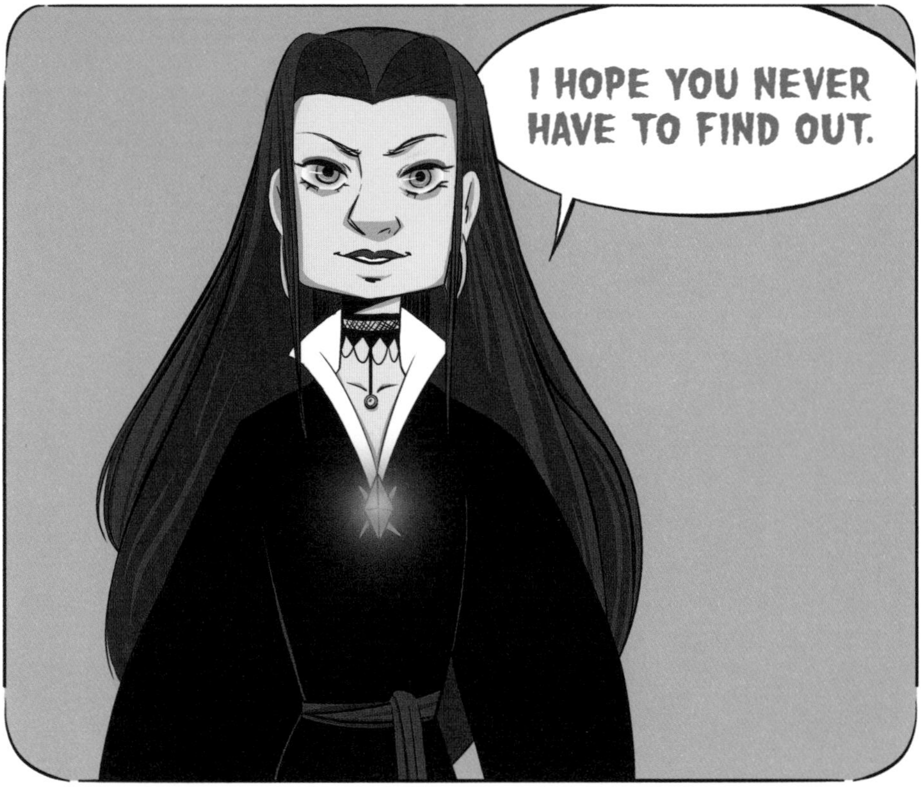
I HOPE YOU NEVER HAVE TO FIND OUT.

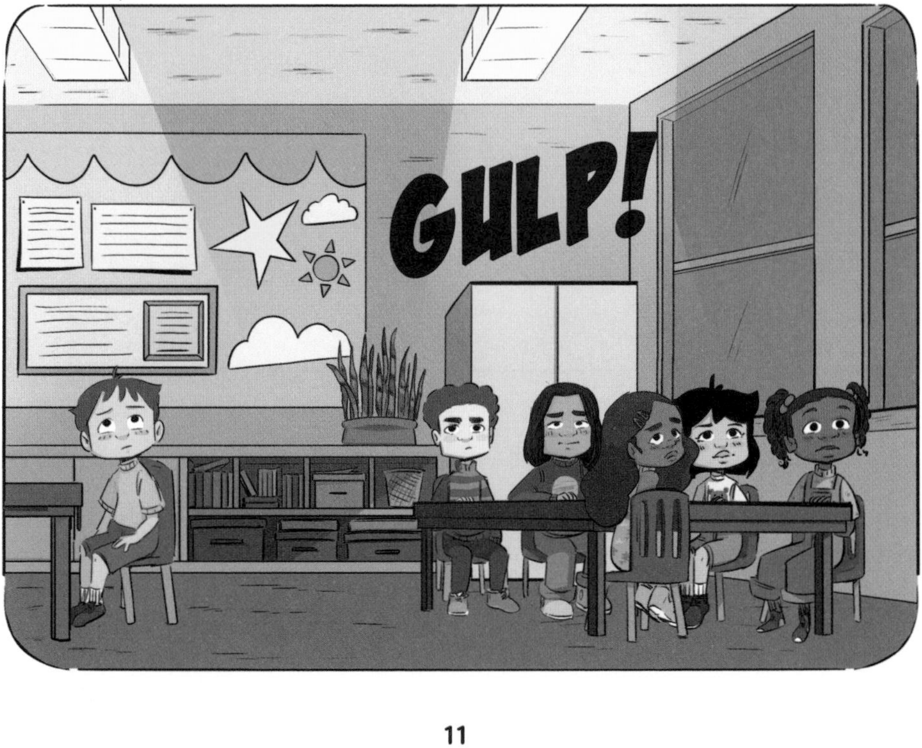
GULP!

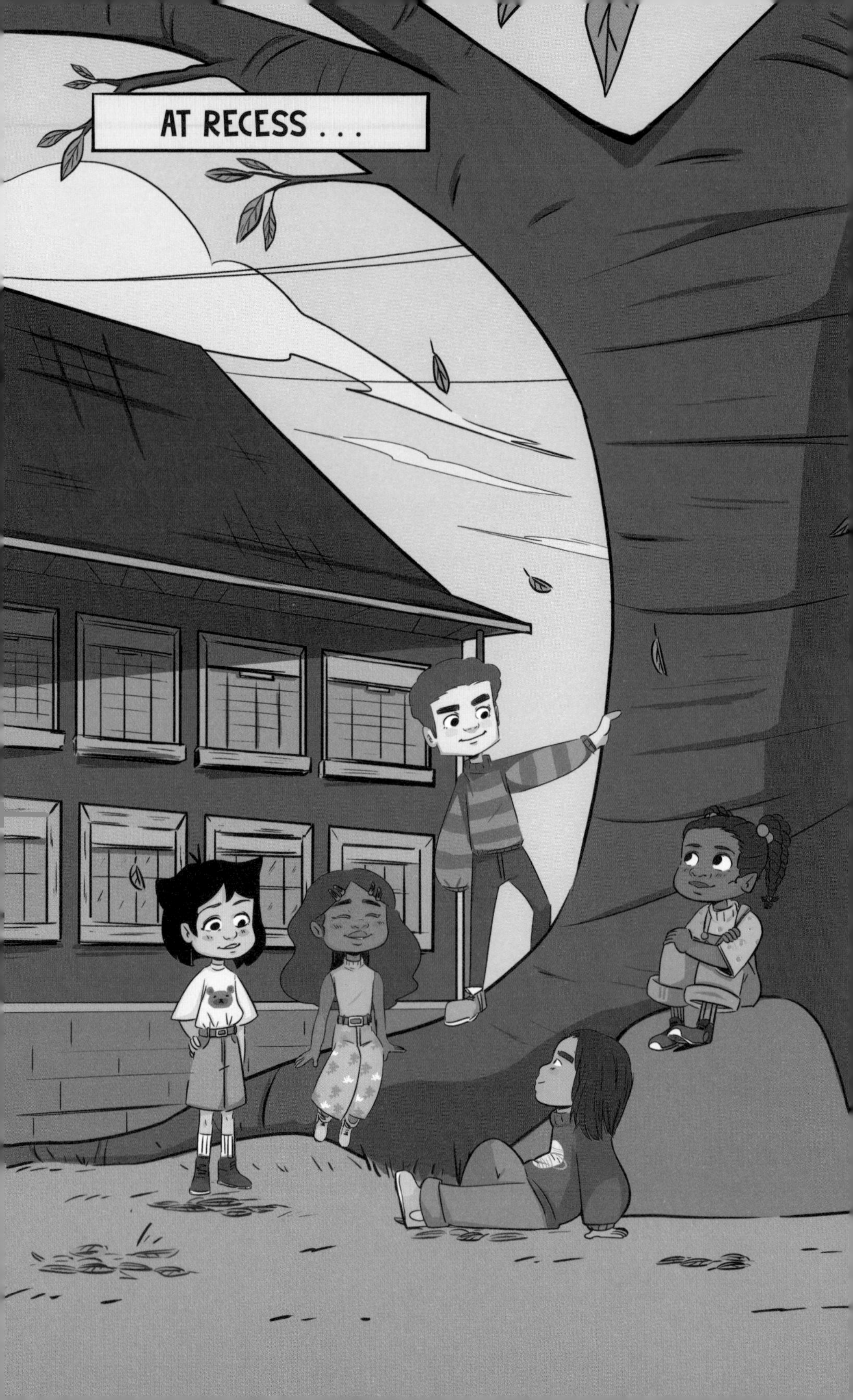
AT RECESS . . .

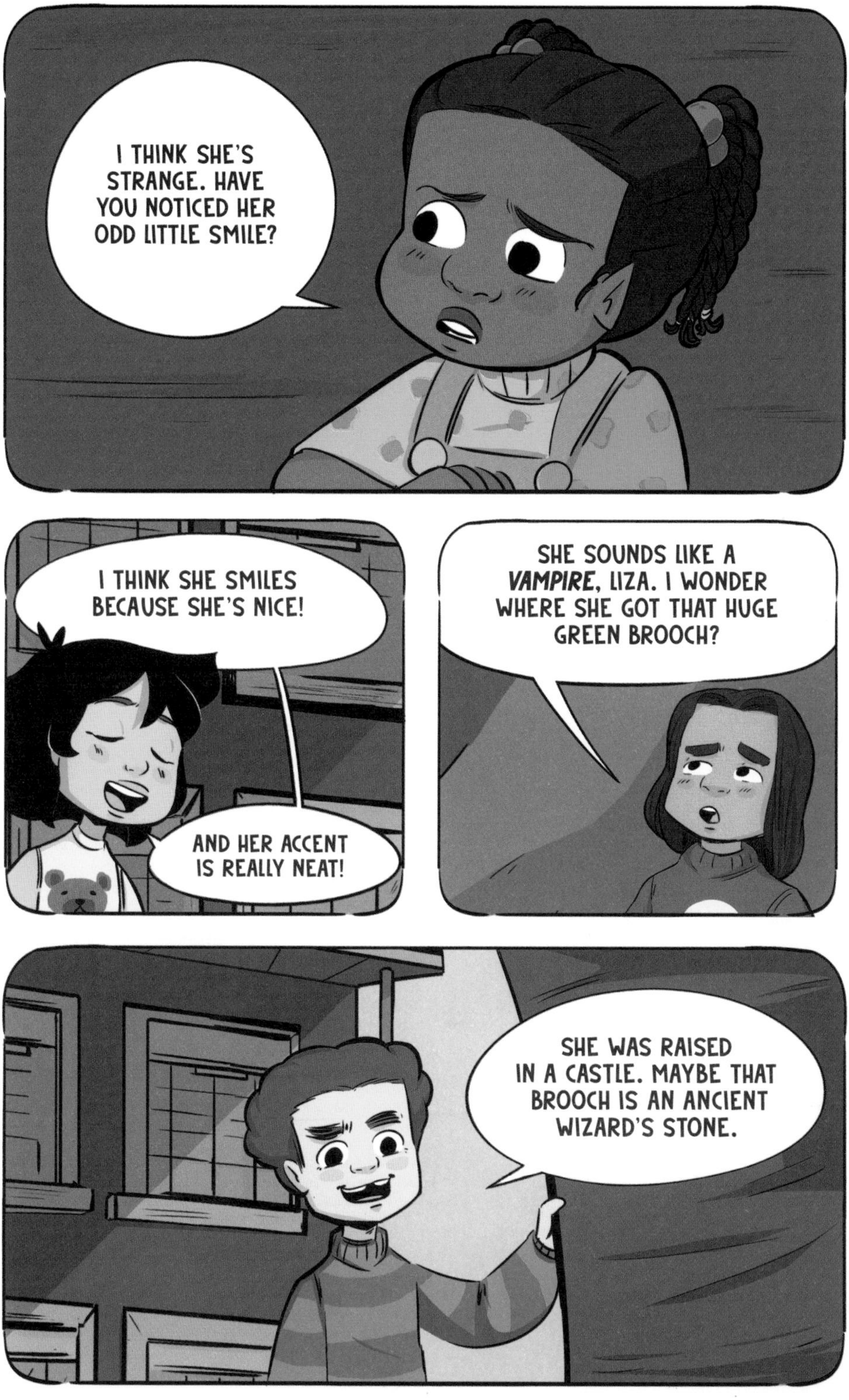
I THINK SHE'S STRANGE. HAVE YOU NOTICED HER ODD LITTLE SMILE?
I THINK SHE SMILES BECAUSE SHE'S NICE!
AND HER ACCENT IS REALLY NEAT!
SHE SOUNDS LIKE A *VAMPIRE*, LIZA. I WONDER WHERE SHE GOT THAT HUGE GREEN BROOCH?
SHE WAS RAISED IN A CASTLE. MAYBE THAT BROOCH IS AN ANCIENT WIZARD'S STONE.

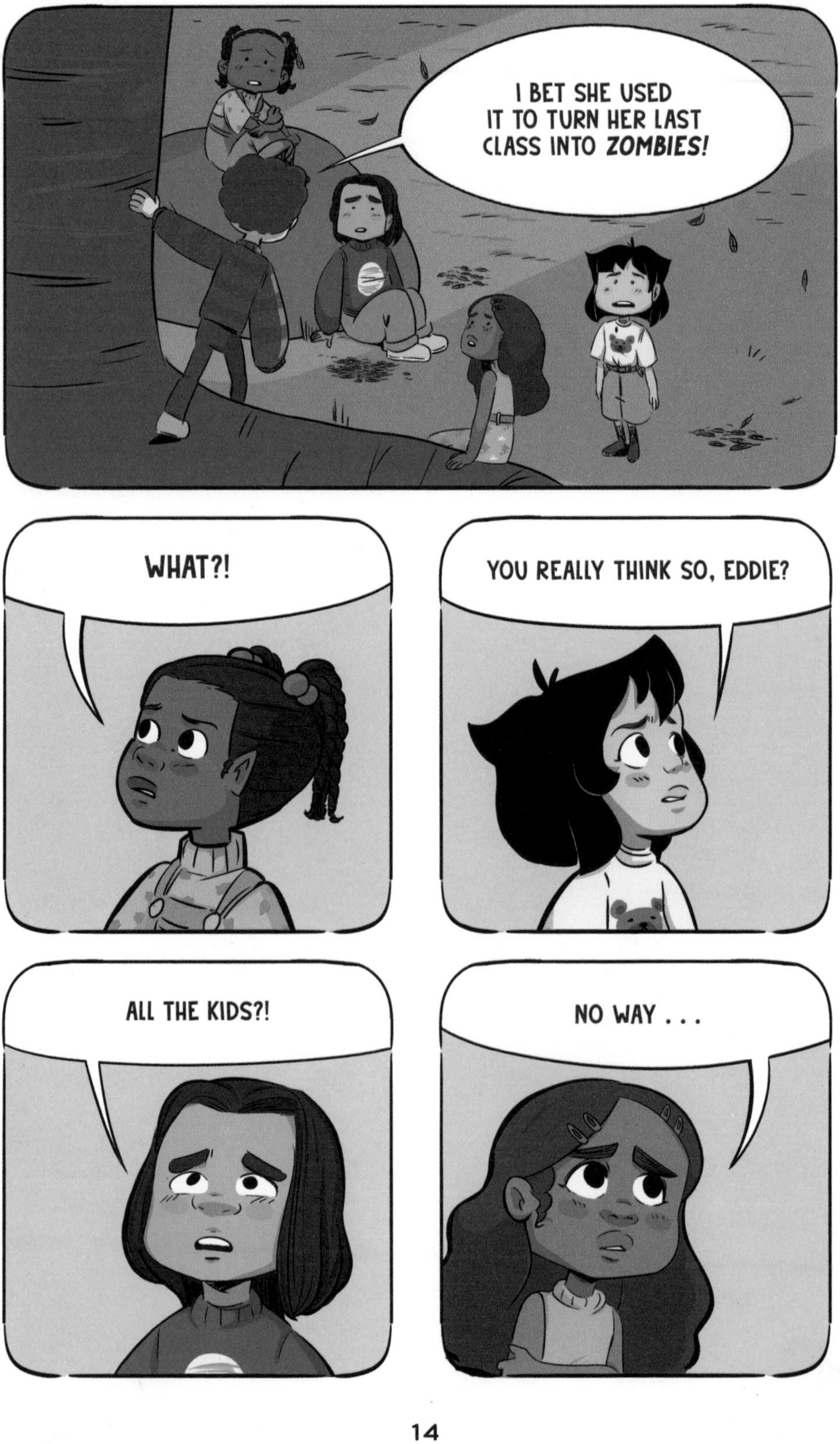
I BET SHE USED IT TO TURN HER LAST CLASS INTO ***ZOMBIES!***
WHAT?!
YOU REALLY THINK SO, EDDIE?
ALL THE KIDS?!
NO WAY . . .

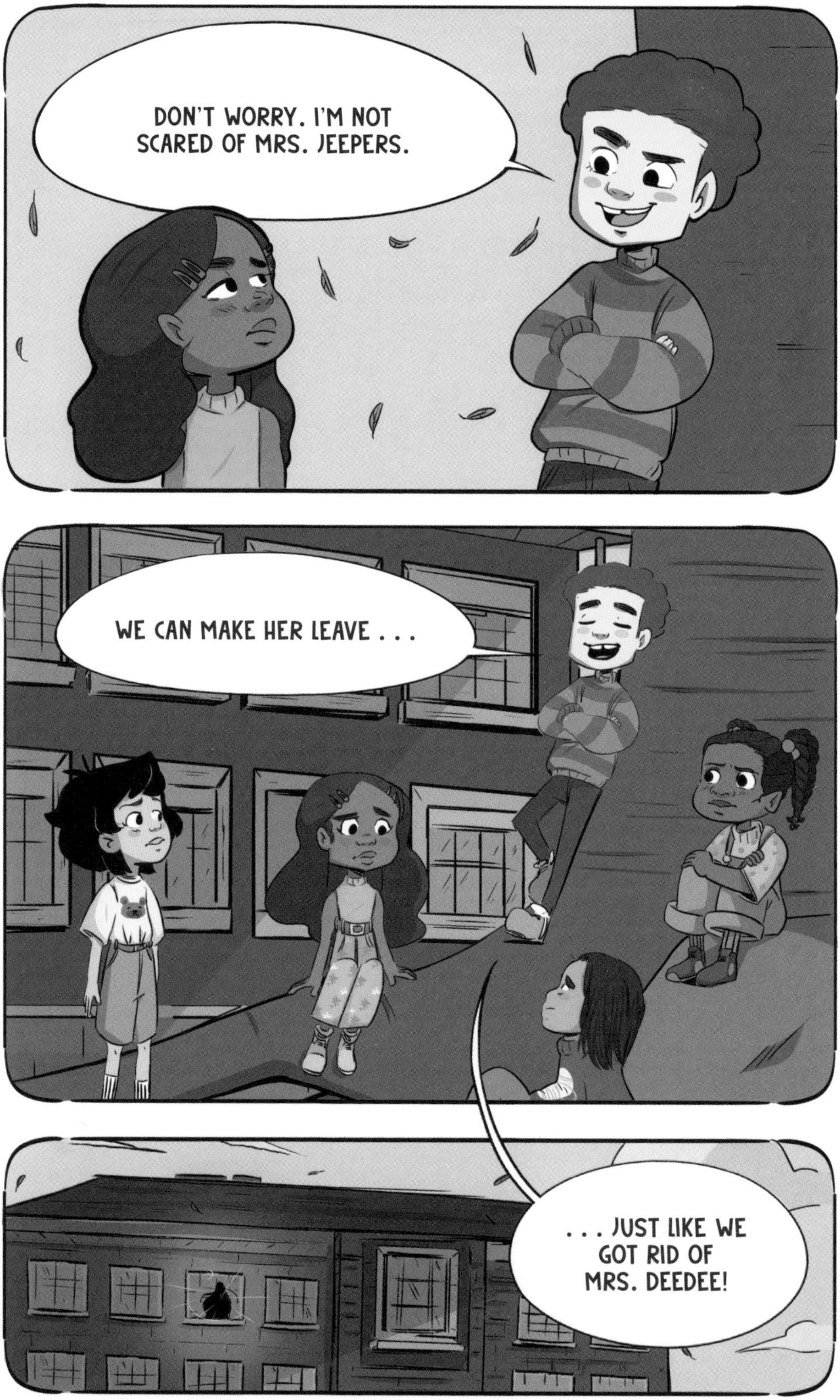
DON'T WORRY. I'M NOT SCARED OF MRS. JEEPERS.
WE CAN MAKE HER LEAVE . . .
. . . JUST LIKE WE GOT RID OF MRS. DEEDEE!

CHAPTER 2 SUSPICIONS

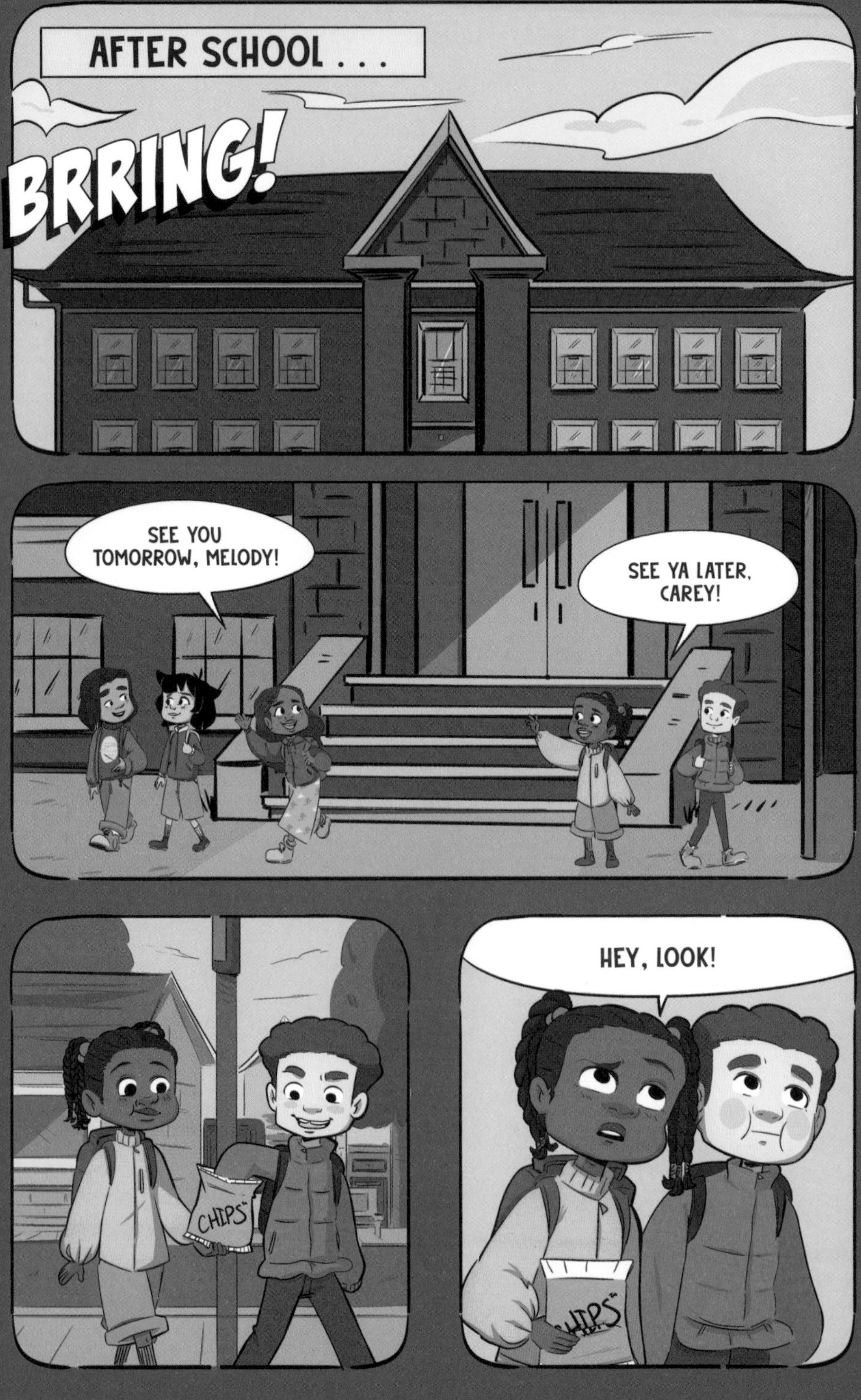
AFTER SCHOOL . . .
BRRING!
SEE YOU TOMORROW, MELODY!
SEE YA LATER, CAREY!
CHIPS
HEY, LOOK!
CHIPS

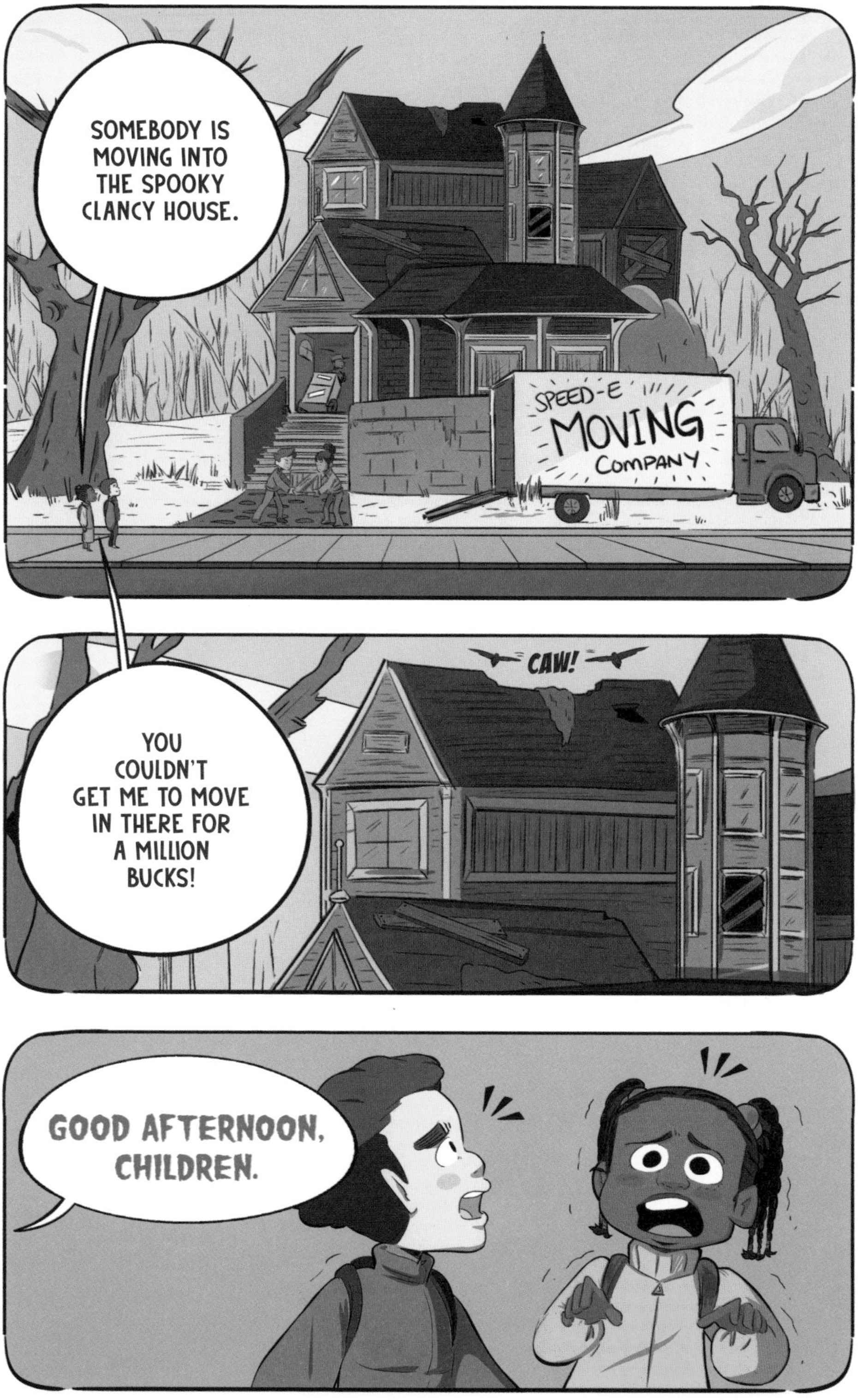
SOMEBODY IS MOVING INTO THE SPOOKY CLANCY HOUSE.
SPEED-E MOVING COMPANY
YOU COULDN'T GET ME TO MOVE IN THERE FOR A MILLION BUCKS!
CAW!
GOOD AFTERNOON, CHILDREN.

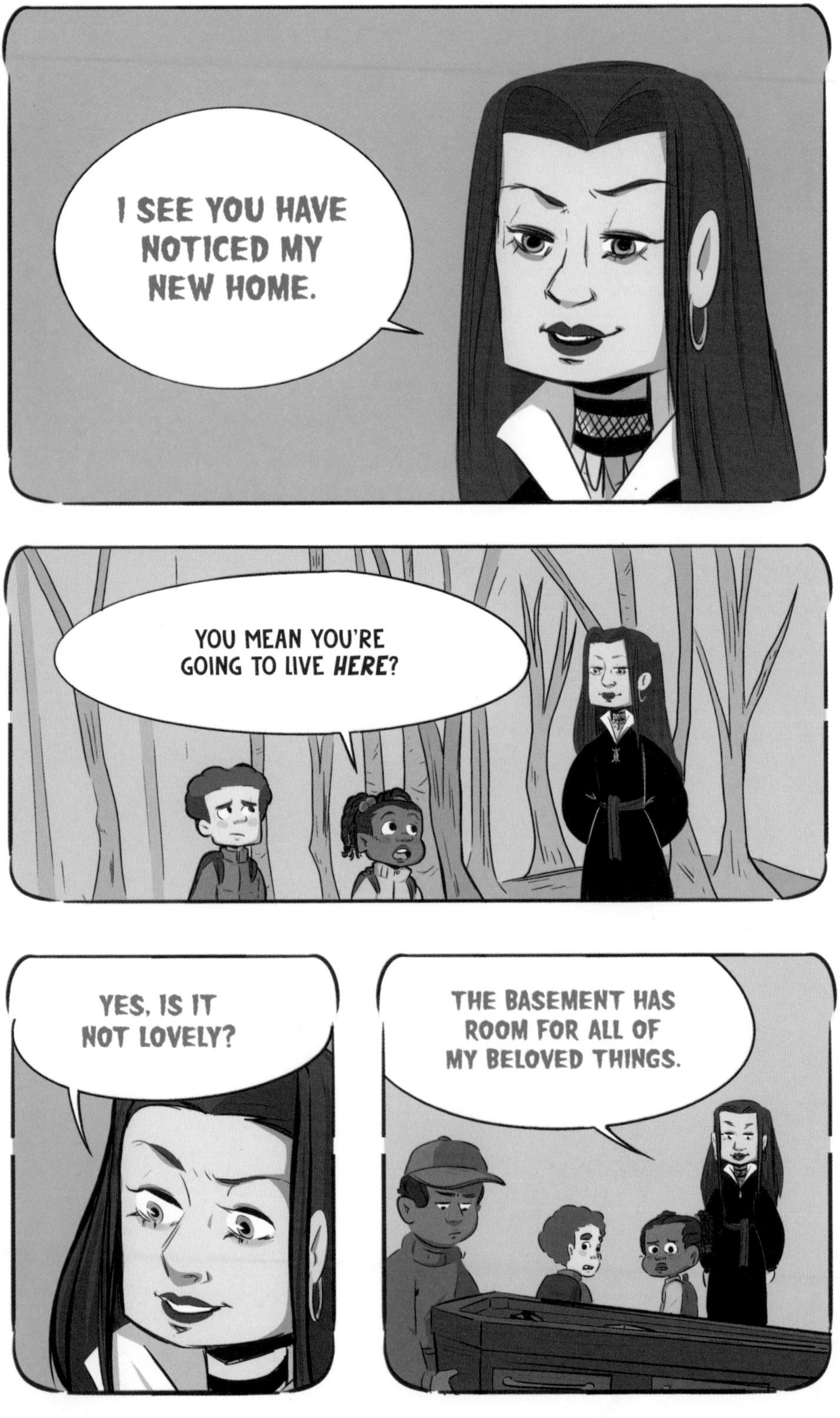
I SEE YOU HAVE NOTICED MY NEW HOME.
YOU MEAN YOU'RE GOING TO LIVE *HERE*?
YES, IS IT NOT LOVELY?
THE BASEMENT HAS ROOM FOR ALL OF MY BELOVED THINGS.

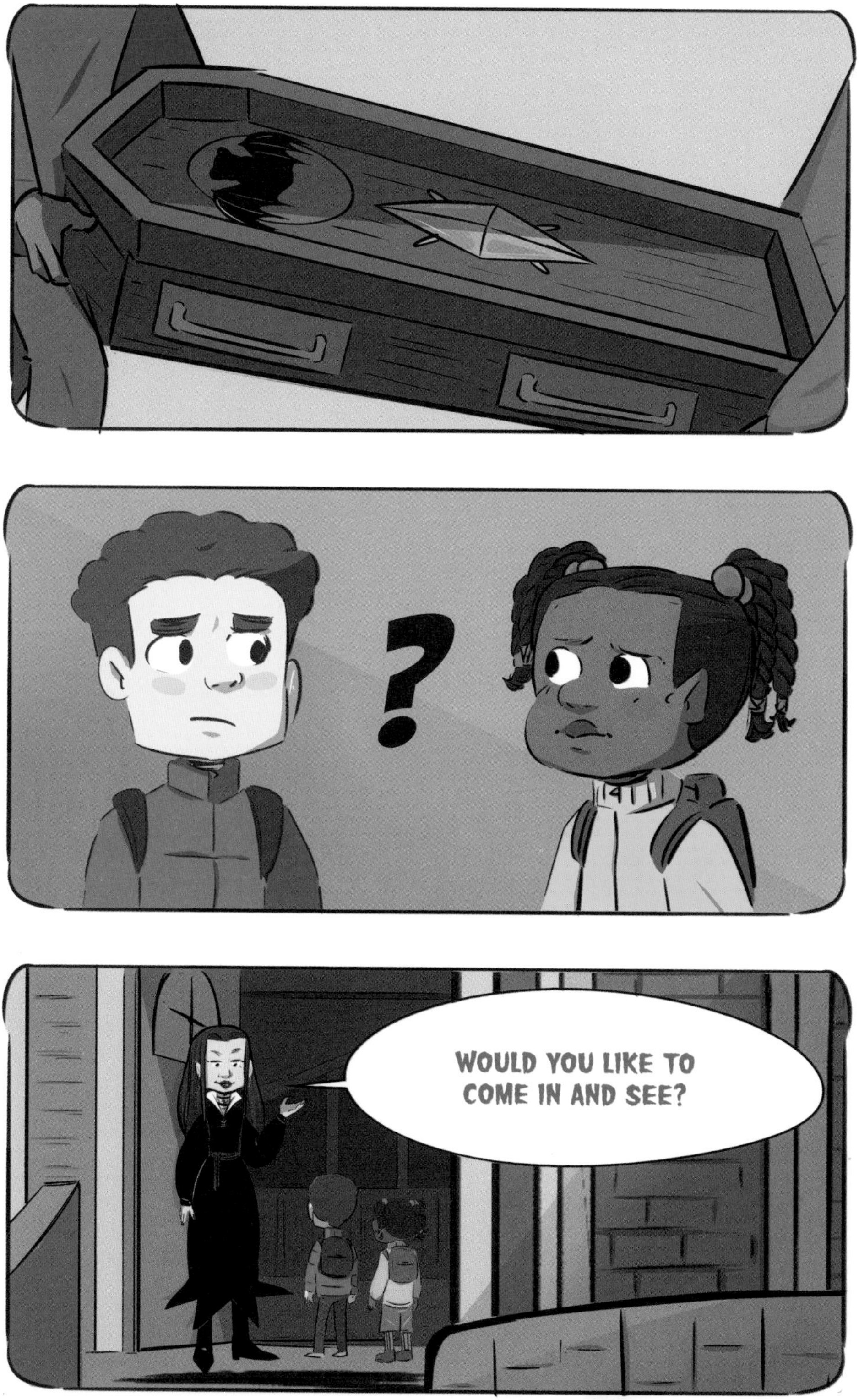
?
WOULD YOU LIKE TO COME IN AND SEE?

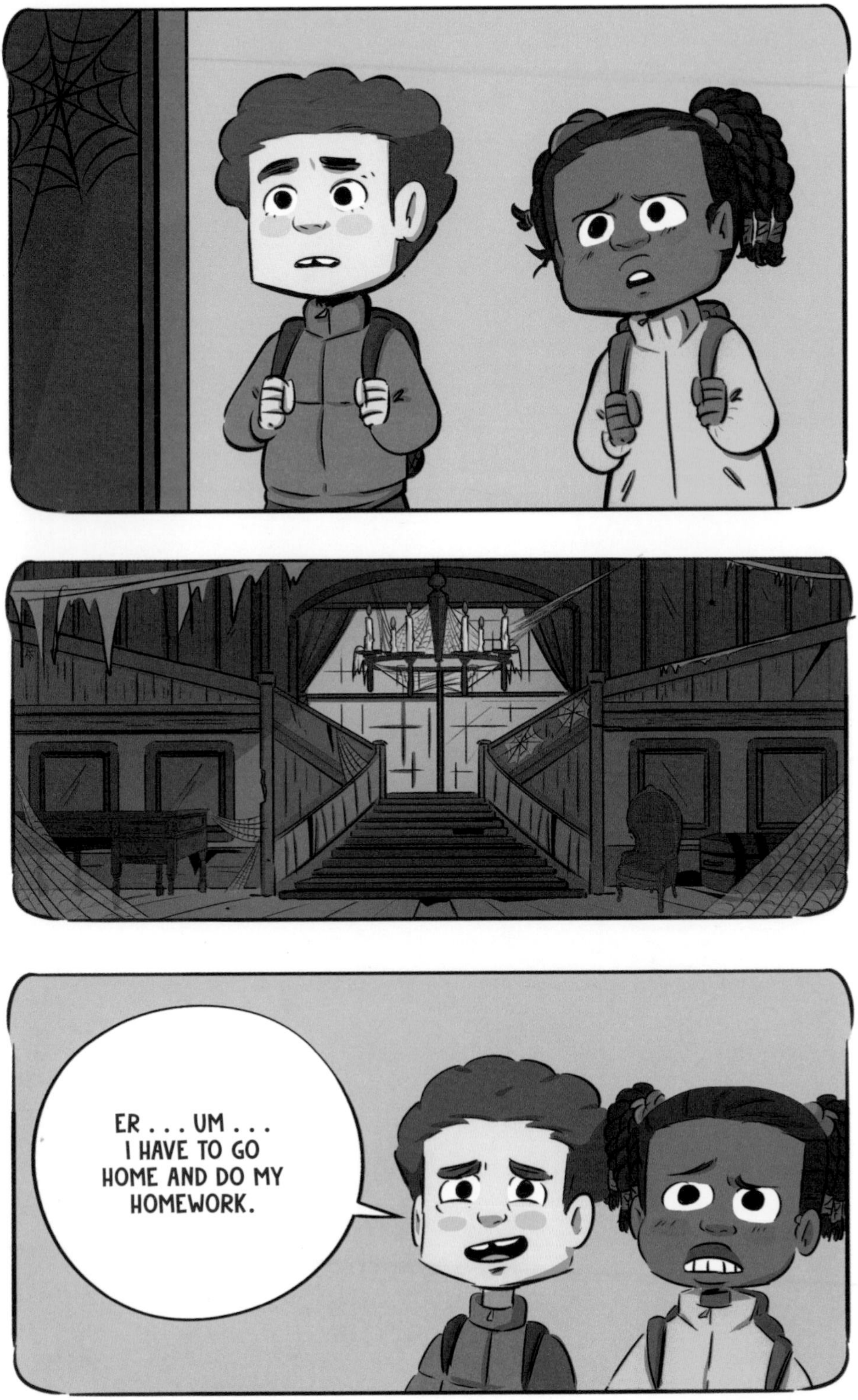
ER . . . UM . . .
I HAVE TO GO
HOME AND DO MY
HOMEWORK.

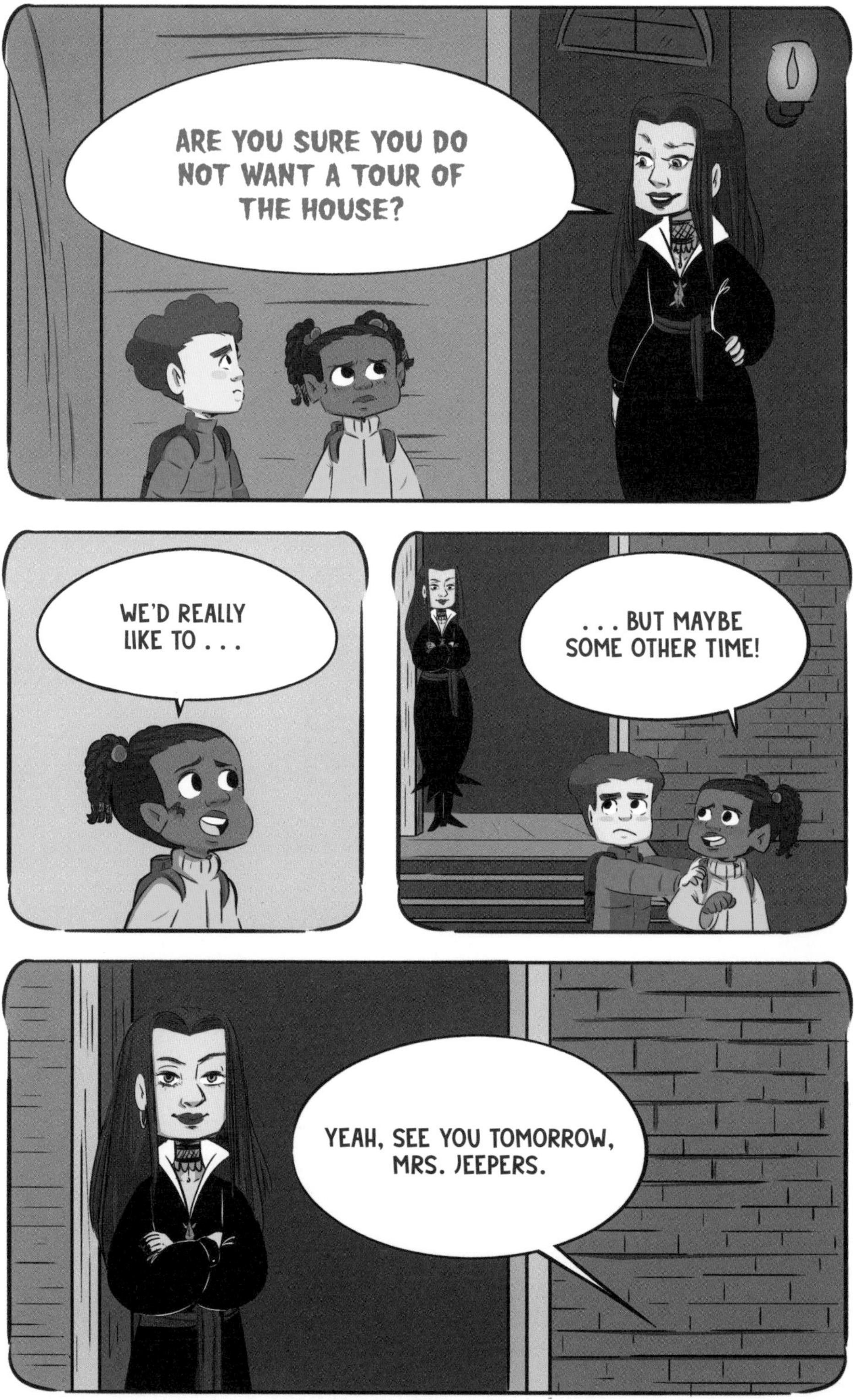
ARE YOU SURE YOU DO NOT WANT A TOUR OF THE HOUSE?
WE'D REALLY LIKE TO . . .
. . . BUT MAYBE SOME OTHER TIME!
YEAH, SEE YOU TOMORROW, MRS. JEEPERS.

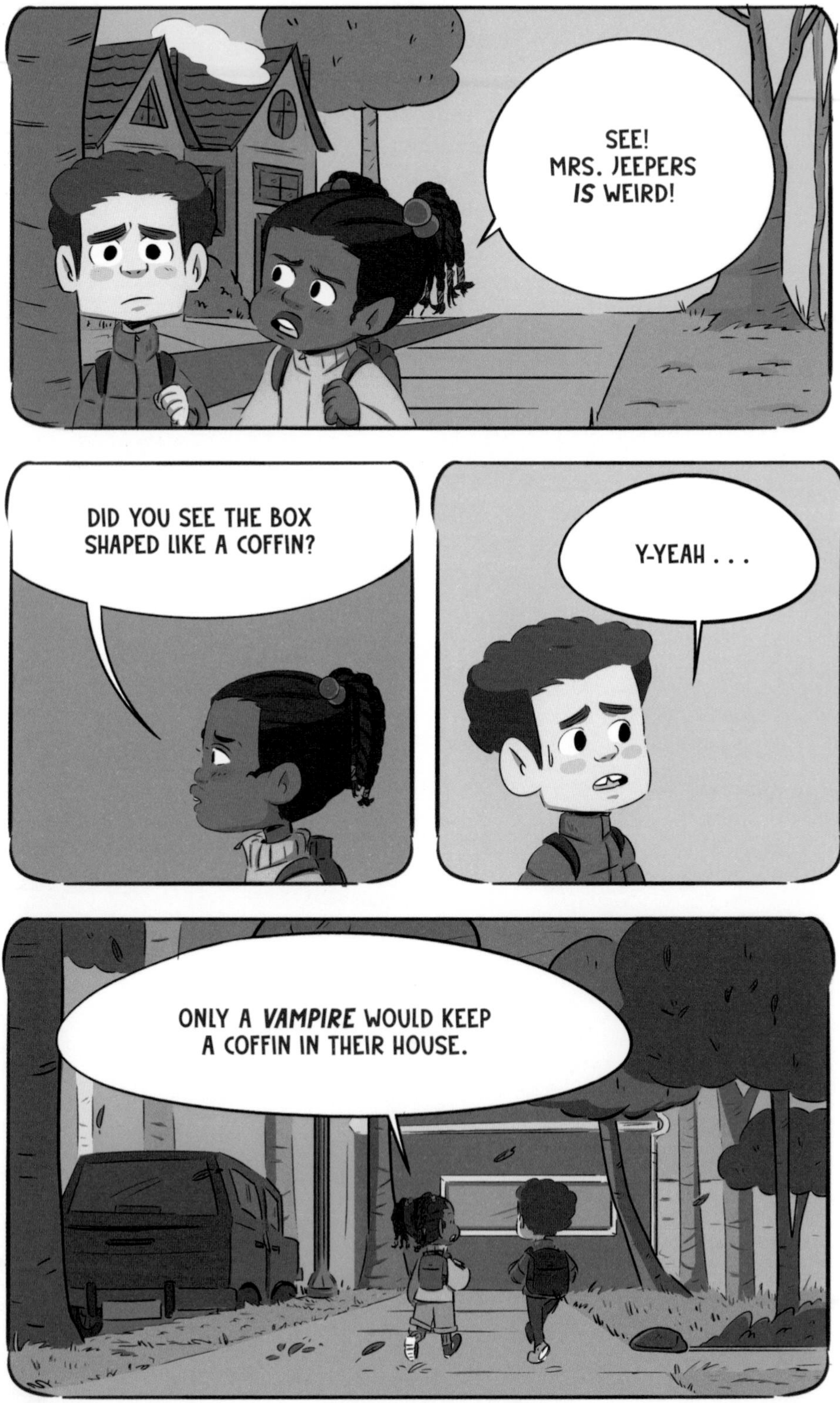
SEE!
MRS. JEEPERS
IS WEIRD!
DID YOU SEE THE BOX
SHAPED LIKE A COFFIN?
Y-YEAH . . .
ONLY A *VAMPIRE* WOULD KEEP
A COFFIN IN THEIR HOUSE.

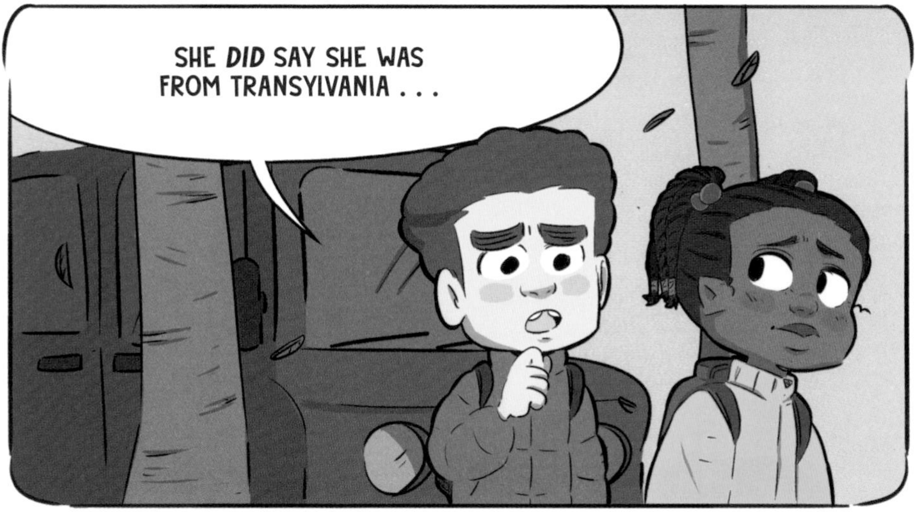
SHE *DID* SAY SHE WAS FROM TRANSYLVANIA . . .

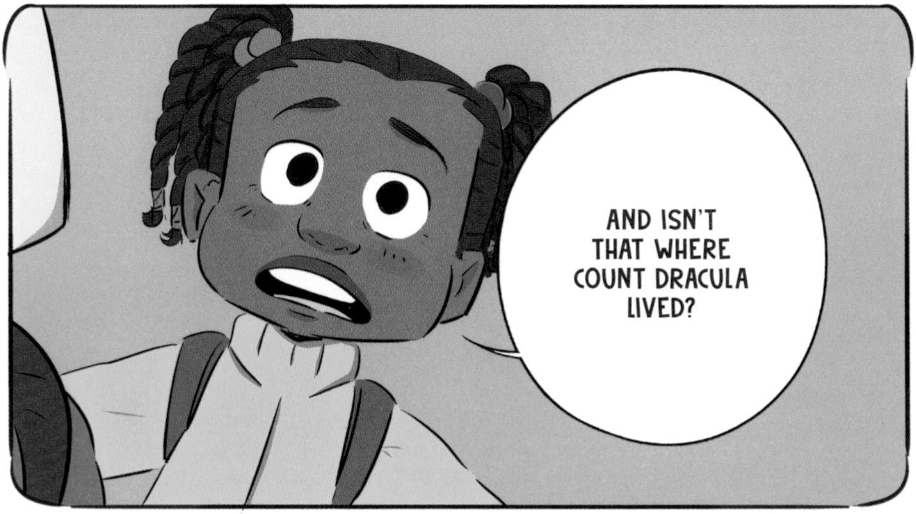
AND ISN'T THAT WHERE COUNT DRACULA LIVED?

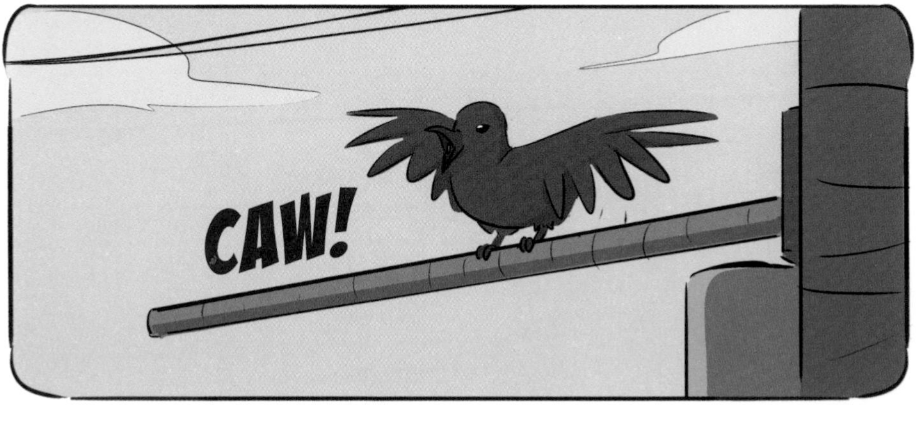
CAW!

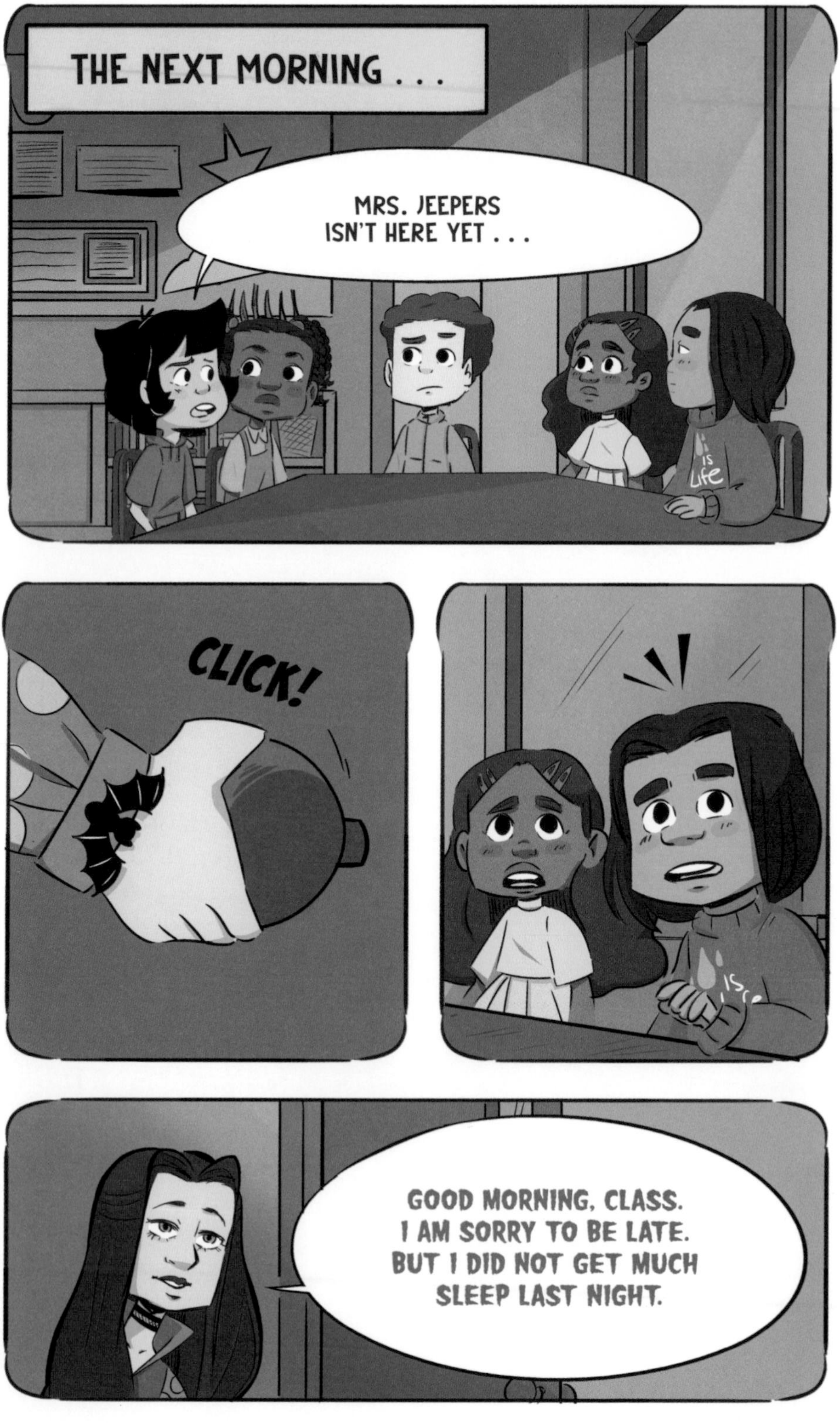
THE NEXT MORNING . . .
MRS. JEEPERS ISN'T HERE YET . . .
CLICK!
GOOD MORNING, CLASS. I AM SORRY TO BE LATE. BUT I DID NOT GET MUCH SLEEP LAST NIGHT.

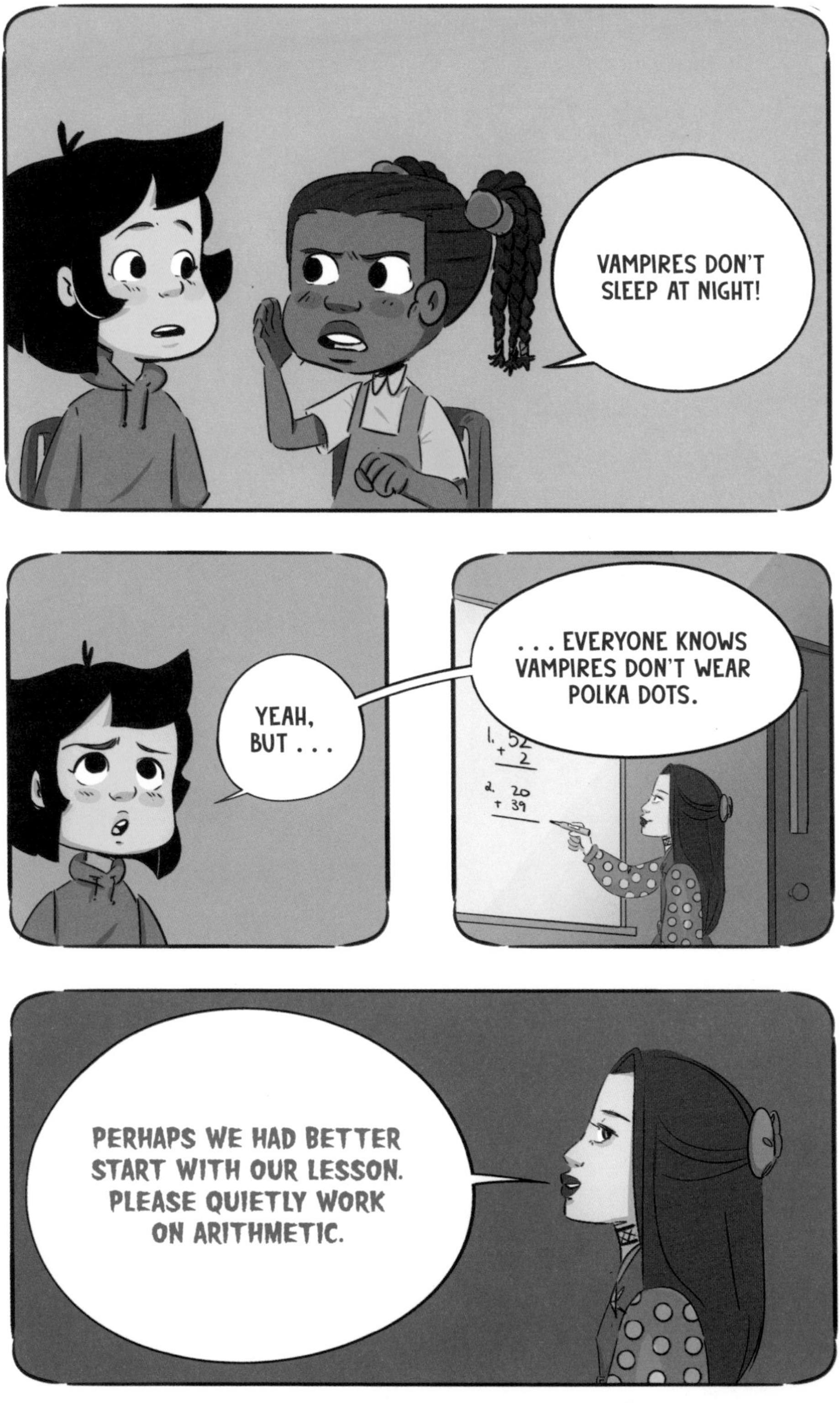
VAMPIRES DON'T SLEEP AT NIGHT!
YEAH, BUT . . .
. . . EVERYONE KNOWS VAMPIRES DON'T WEAR POLKA DOTS.
PERHAPS WE HAD BETTER START WITH OUR LESSON. PLEASE QUIETLY WORK ON ARITHMETIC.

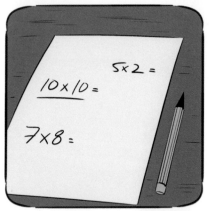

$$5 \times 2 =$$
$$10 \times 10 =$$
$$7 \times 8 =$$

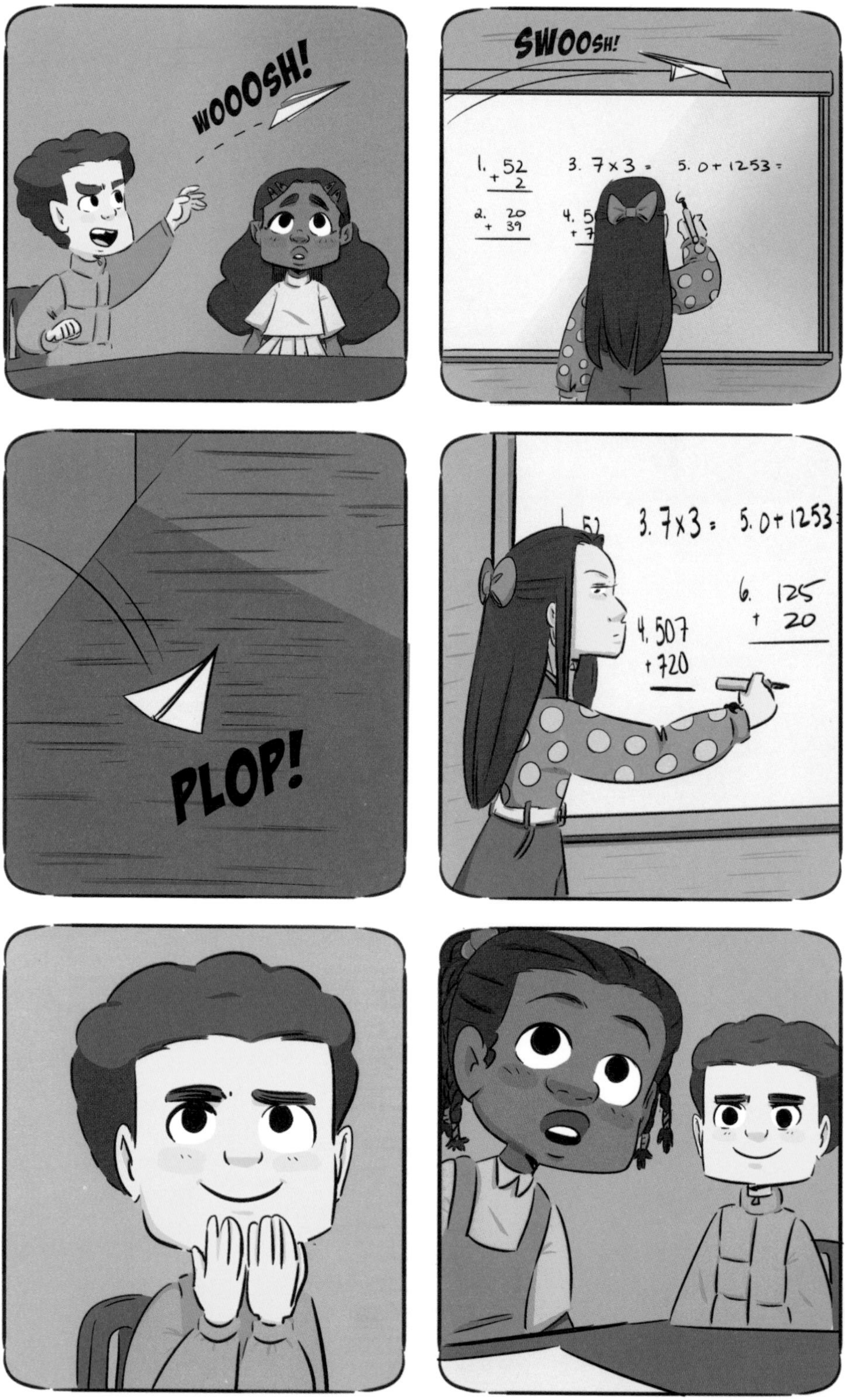
WOOOSH!
SWOOSH!
1. 52 + 2
3. 7×3 =
5. 0+1253 =
2. 20 + 39
PLOP!
4. 507 + 720
6. 125 + 20

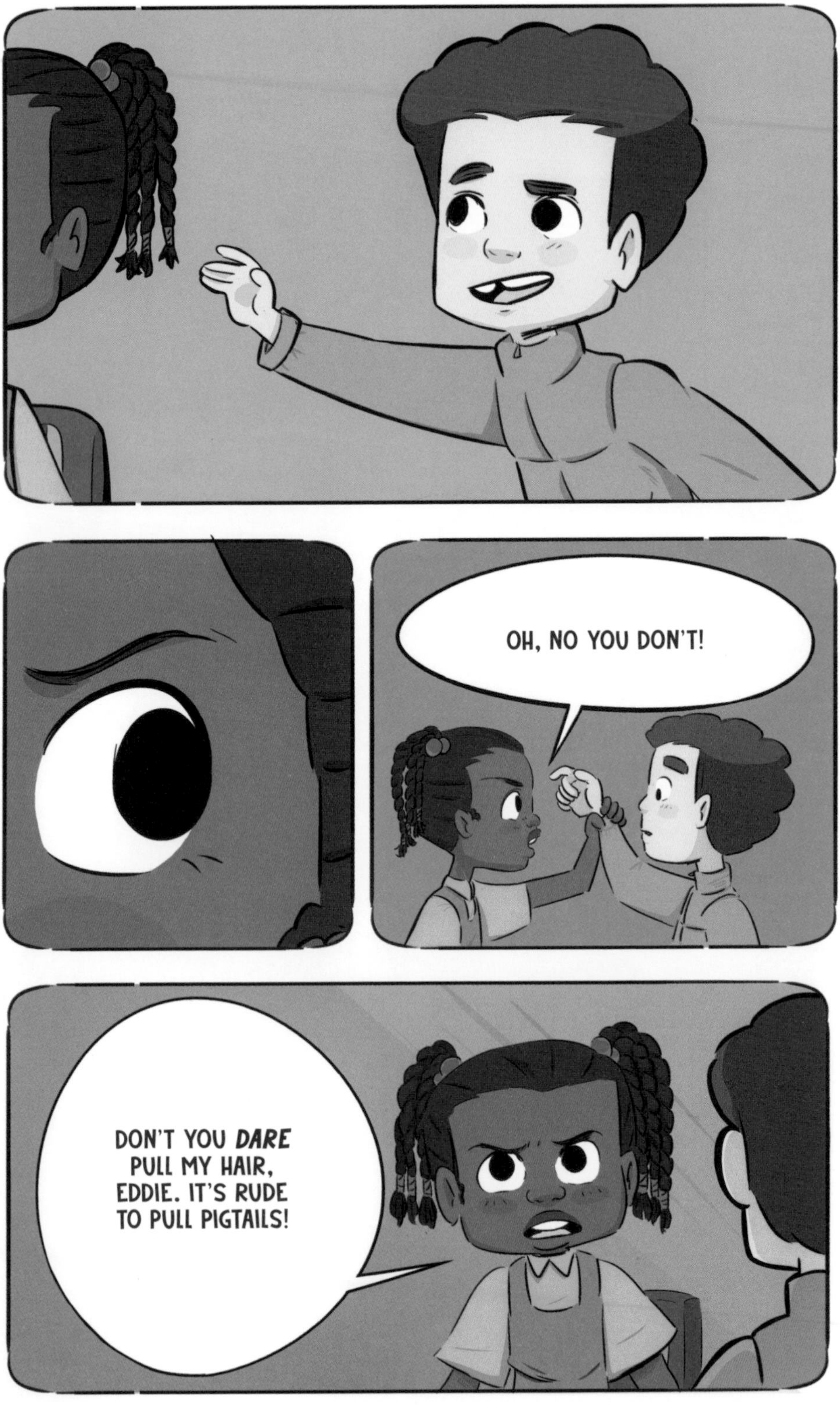
OH, NO YOU DON'T!
DON'T YOU ***DARE*** PULL MY HAIR, EDDIE. IT'S RUDE TO PULL PIGTAILS!

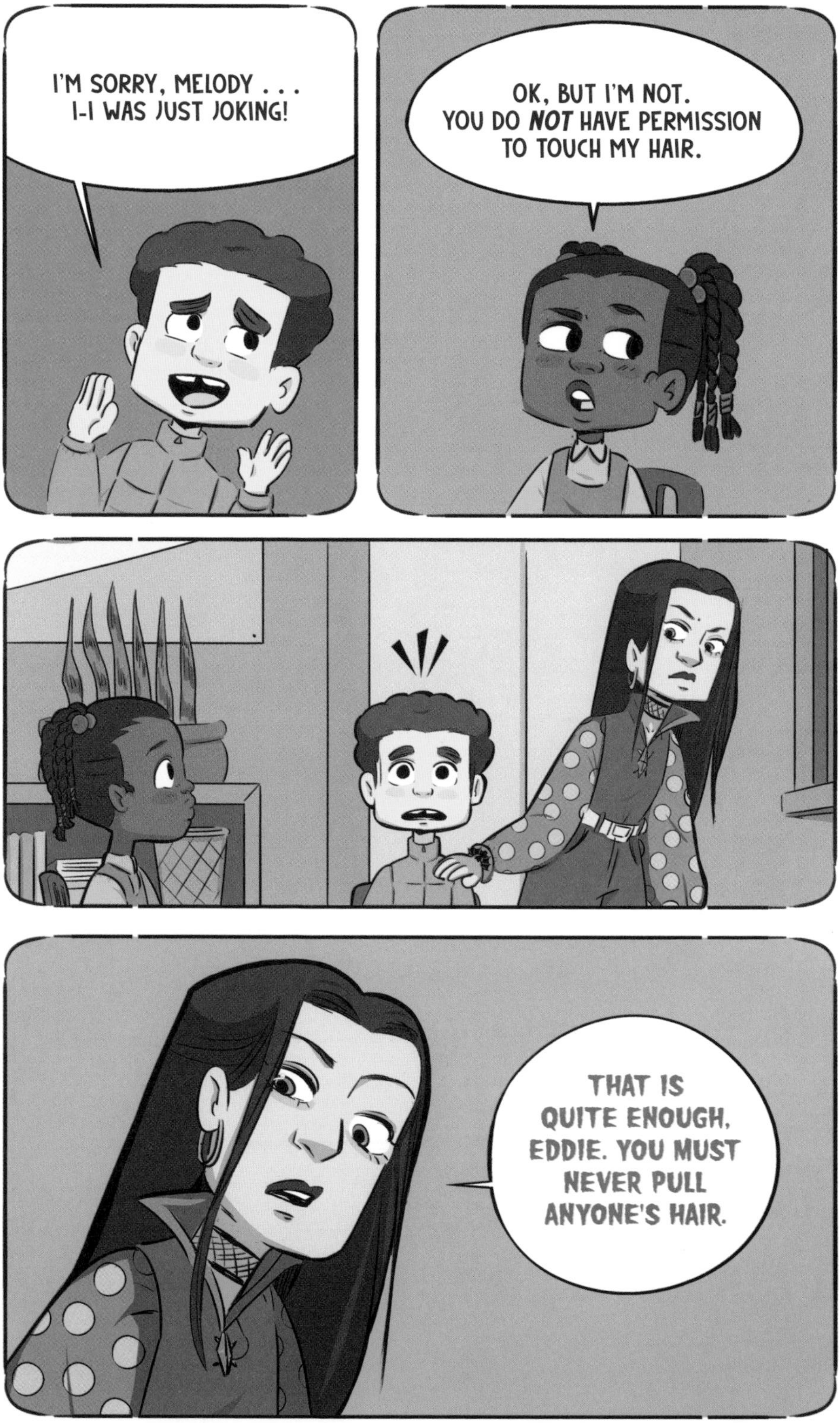
I'M SORRY, MELODY . . .
I-I WAS JUST JOKING!
OK, BUT I'M NOT.
YOU DO ***NOT*** HAVE PERMISSION
TO TOUCH MY HAIR.
THAT IS
QUITE ENOUGH,
EDDIE. YOU MUST
NEVER PULL
ANYONE'S HAIR.

CHAPTER 3 THE DARE

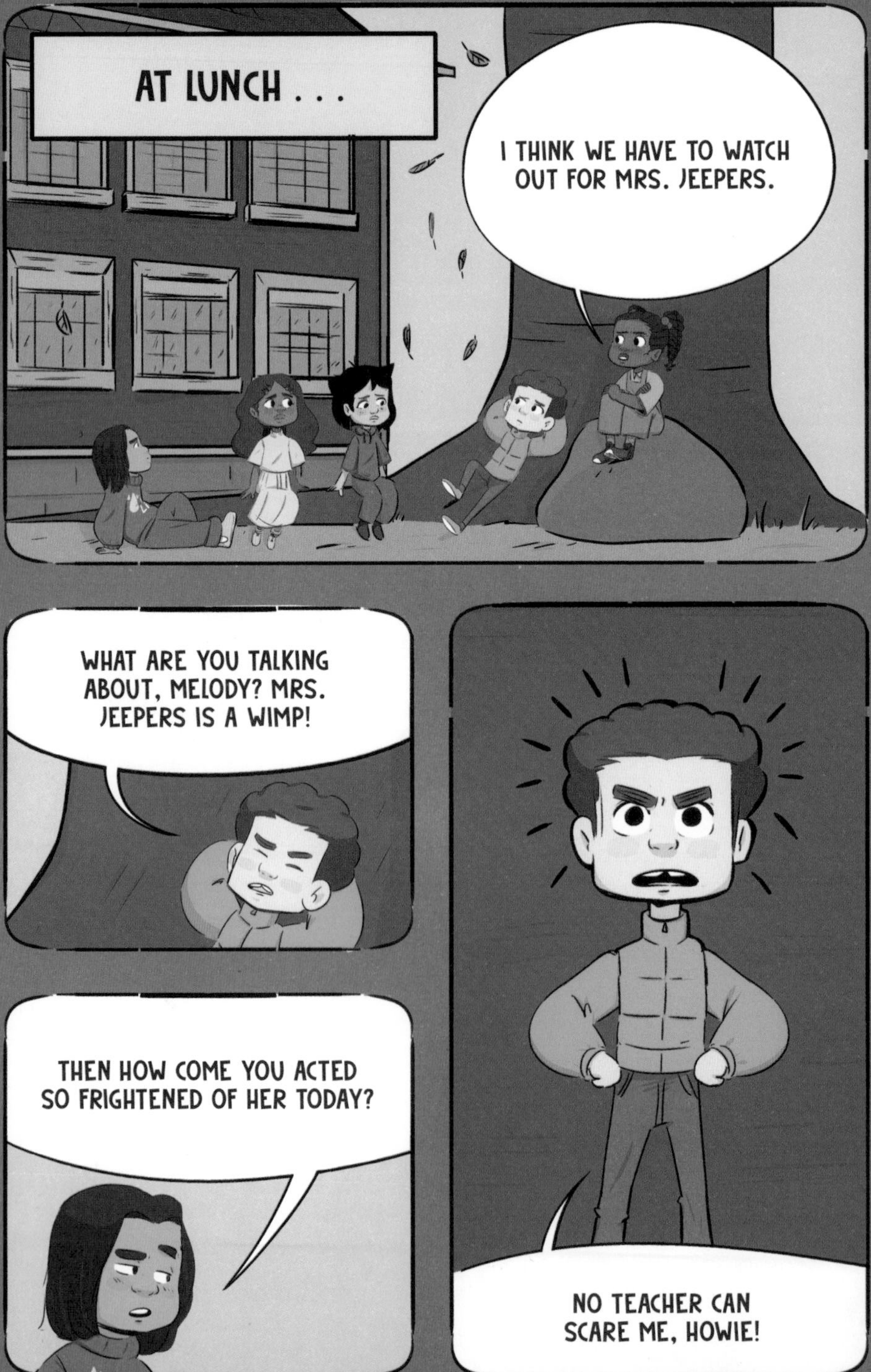
AT LUNCH . . .
I THINK WE HAVE TO WATCH OUT FOR MRS. JEEPERS.
WHAT ARE YOU TALKING ABOUT, MELODY? MRS. JEEPERS IS A WIMP!
THEN HOW COME YOU ACTED SO FRIGHTENED OF HER TODAY?
NO TEACHER CAN SCARE ME, HOWIE!

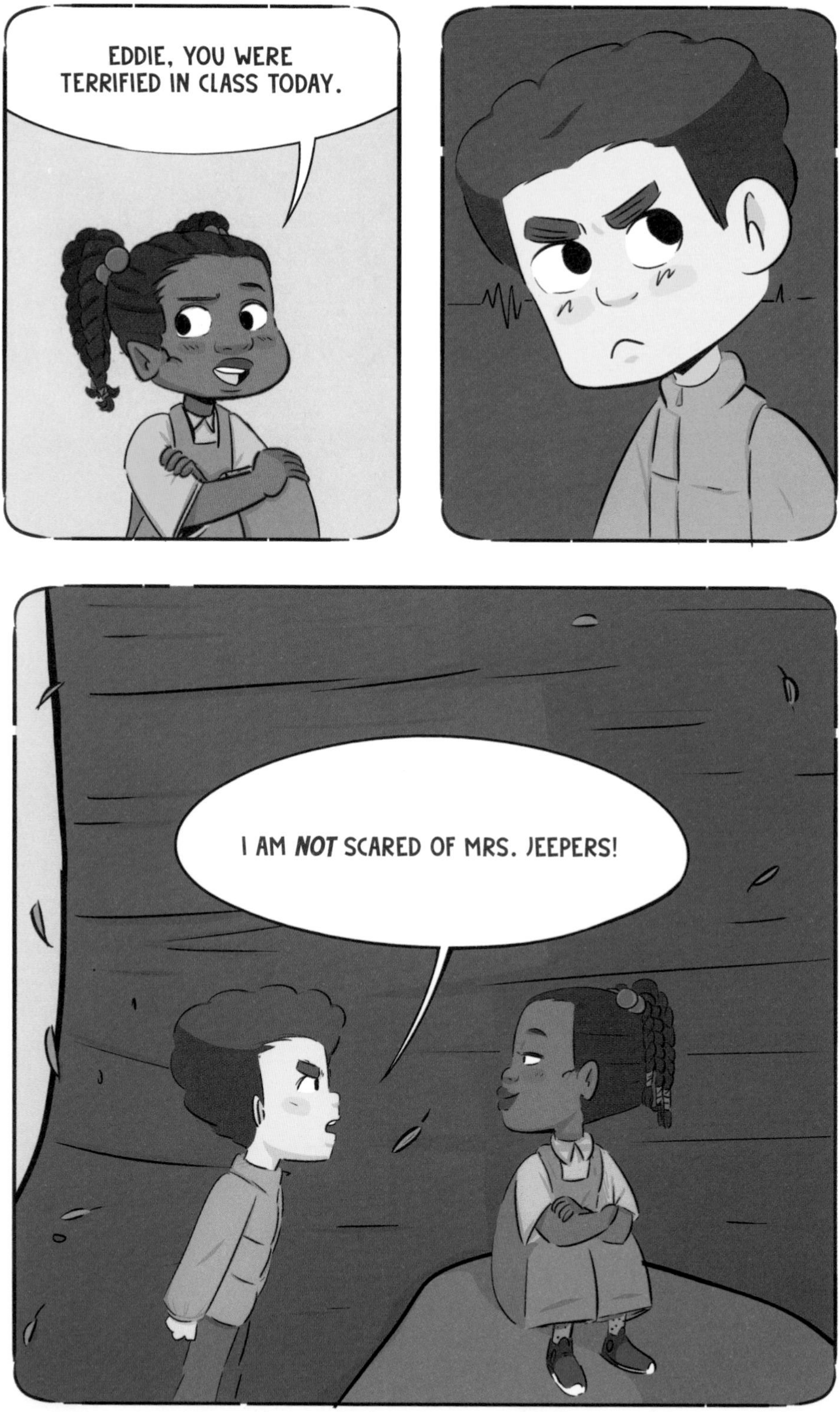
EDDIE, YOU WERE TERRIFIED IN CLASS TODAY.
I AM *NOT* SCARED OF MRS. JEEPERS!

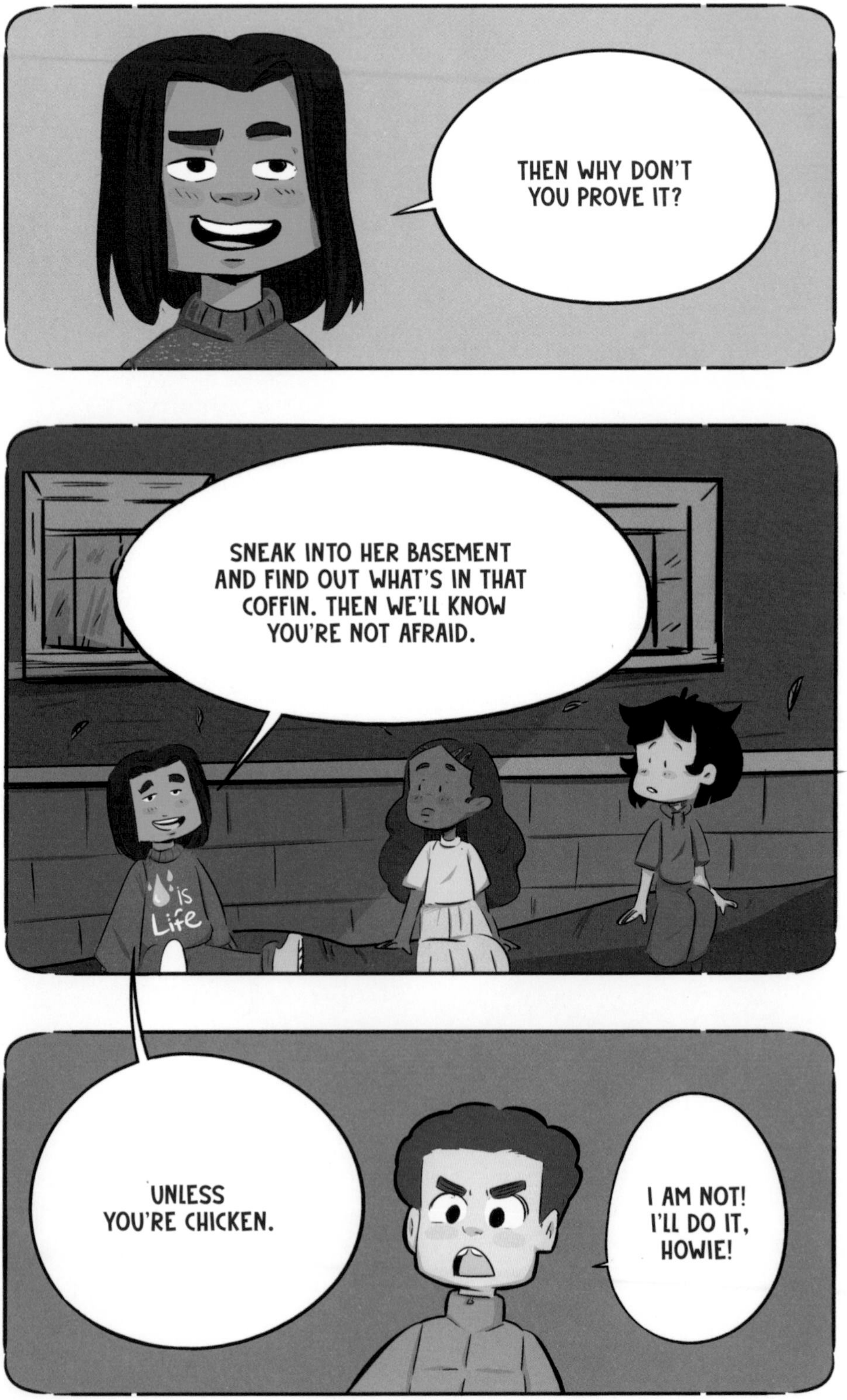
THEN WHY DON'T YOU PROVE IT?
SNEAK INTO HER BASEMENT AND FIND OUT WHAT'S IN THAT COFFIN. THEN WE'LL KNOW YOU'RE NOT AFRAID.
is Life
UNLESS YOU'RE CHICKEN.
I AM NOT! I'LL DO IT, HOWIE!

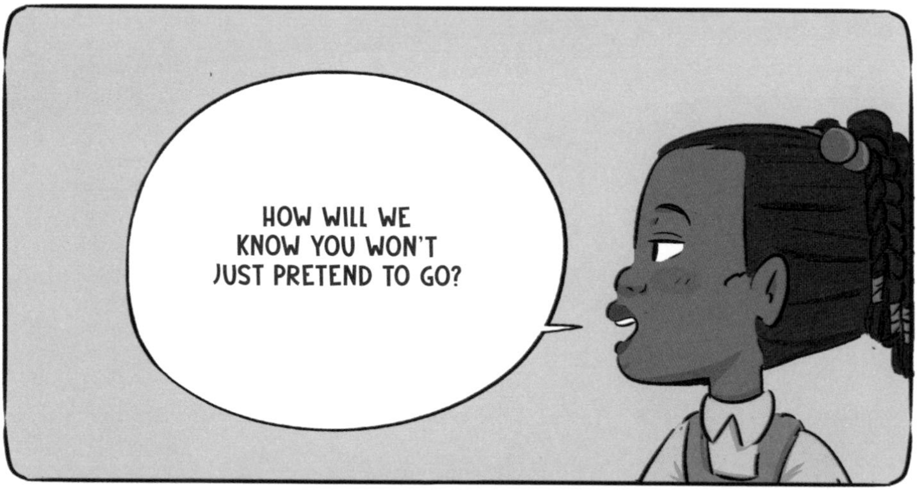
HOW WILL WE KNOW YOU WON'T JUST PRETEND TO GO?

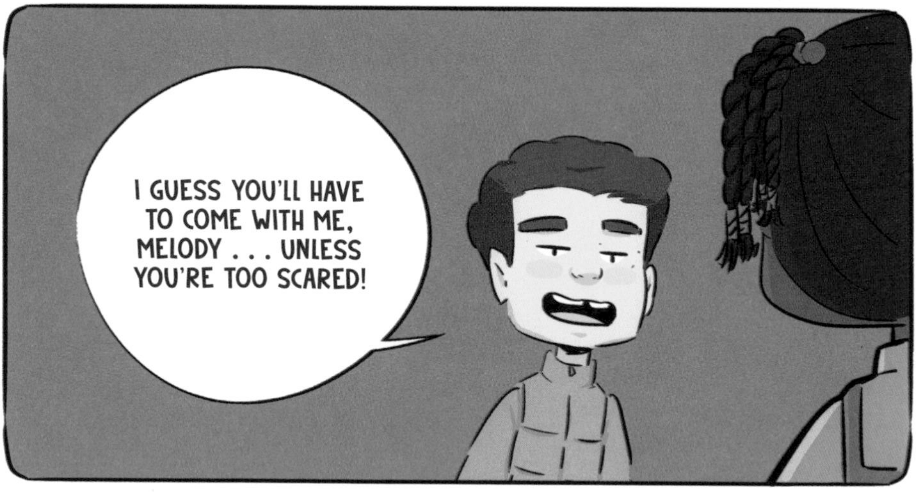
I GUESS YOU'LL HAVE TO COME WITH ME, MELODY . . . UNLESS YOU'RE TOO SCARED!

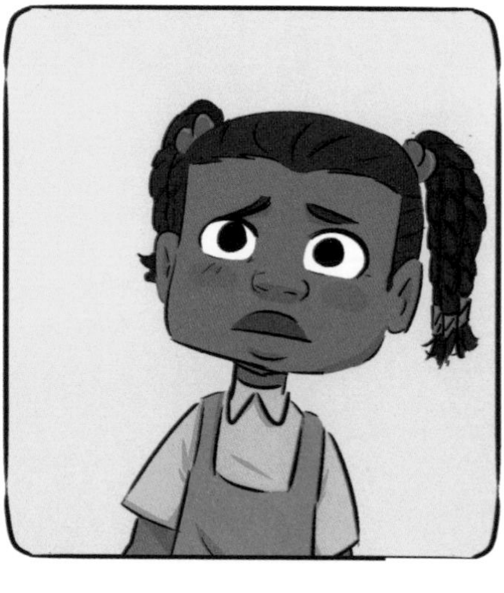

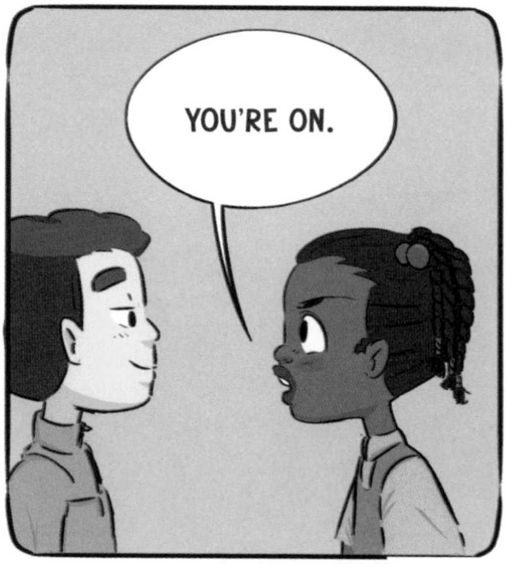
YOU'RE ON.

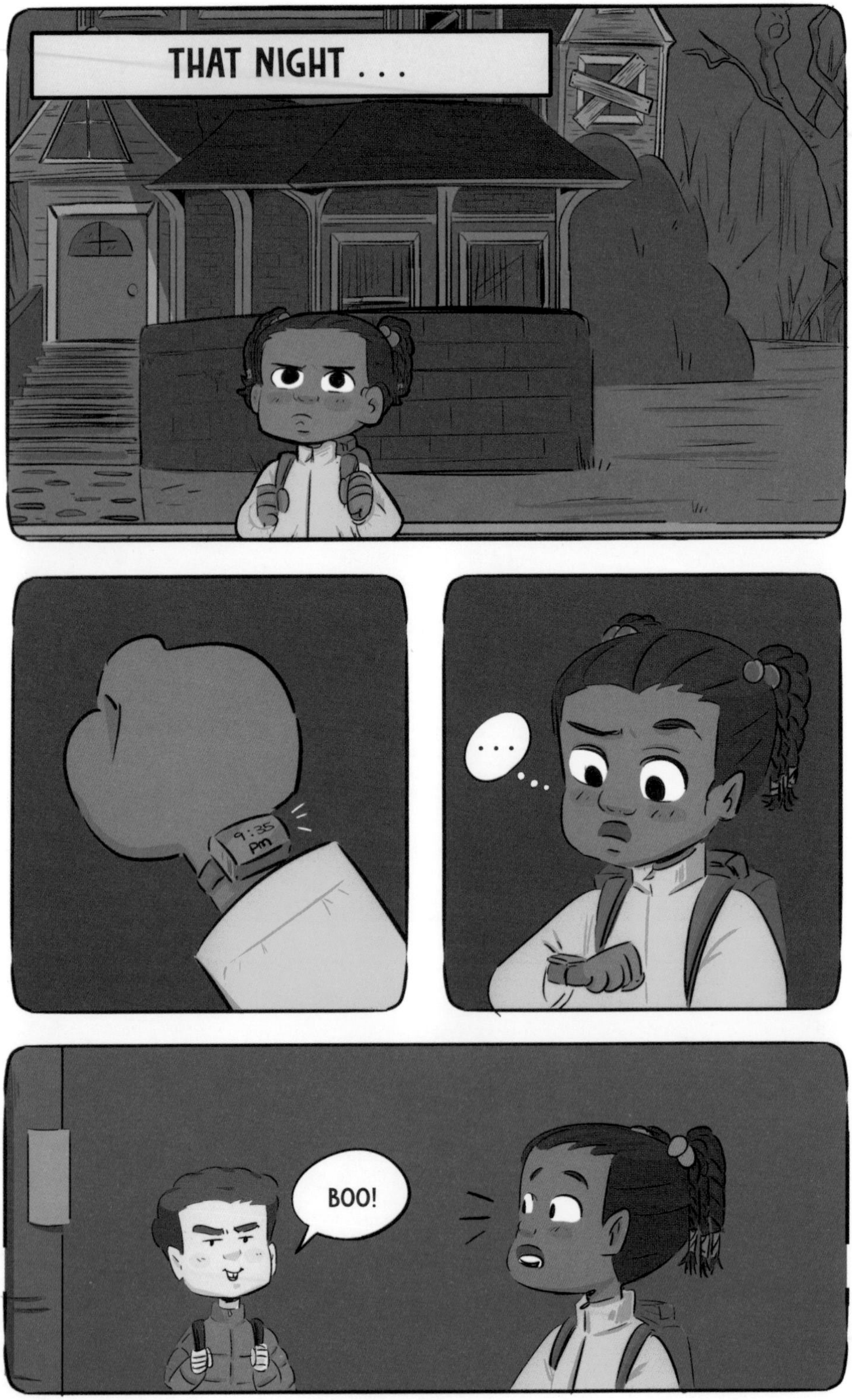
THAT NIGHT . . .
9:35 pm
. . .
BOO!

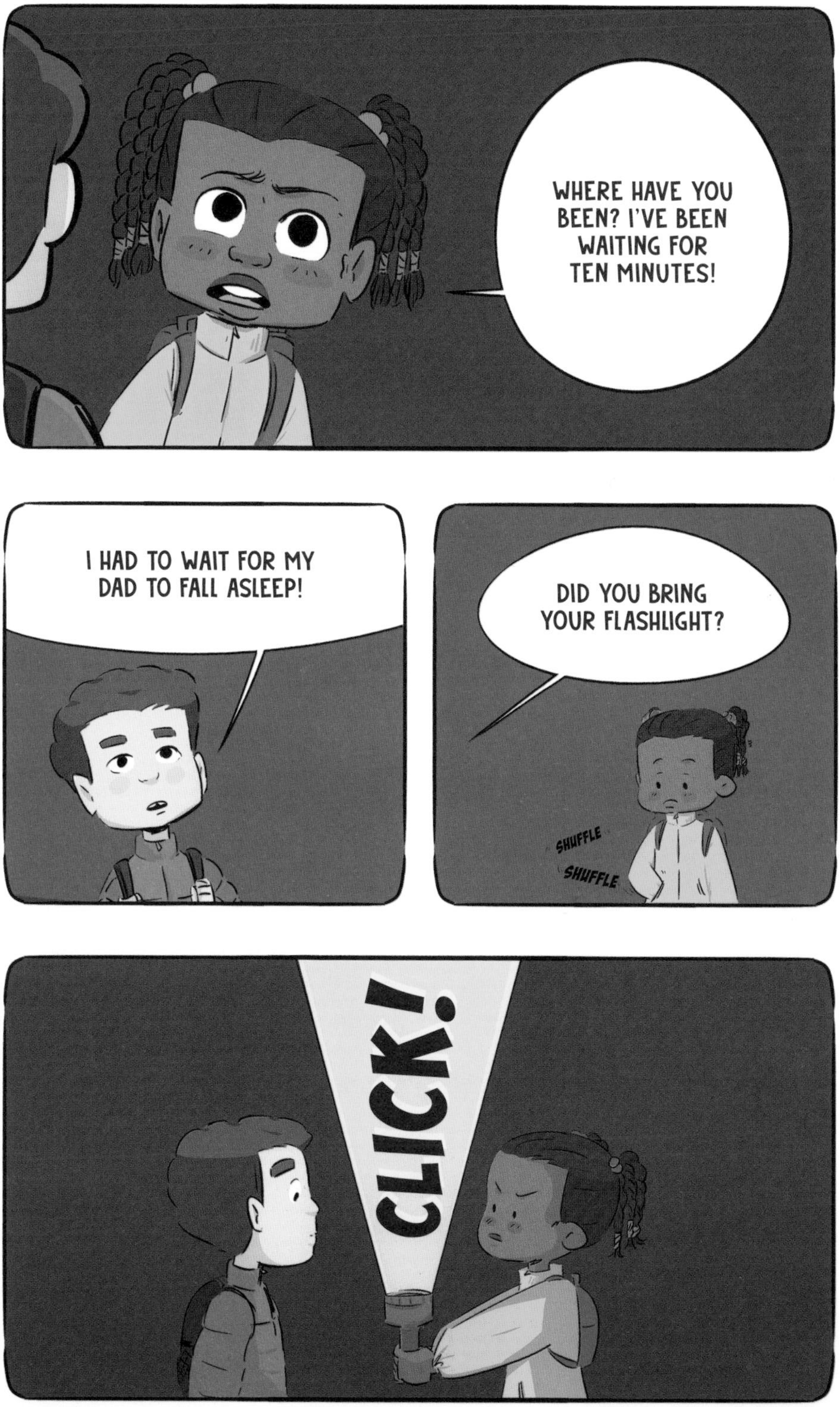
WHERE HAVE YOU BEEN? I'VE BEEN WAITING FOR TEN MINUTES!
I HAD TO WAIT FOR MY DAD TO FALL ASLEEP!
DID YOU BRING YOUR FLASHLIGHT?
SHUFFLE
SHUFFLE
CLICK!

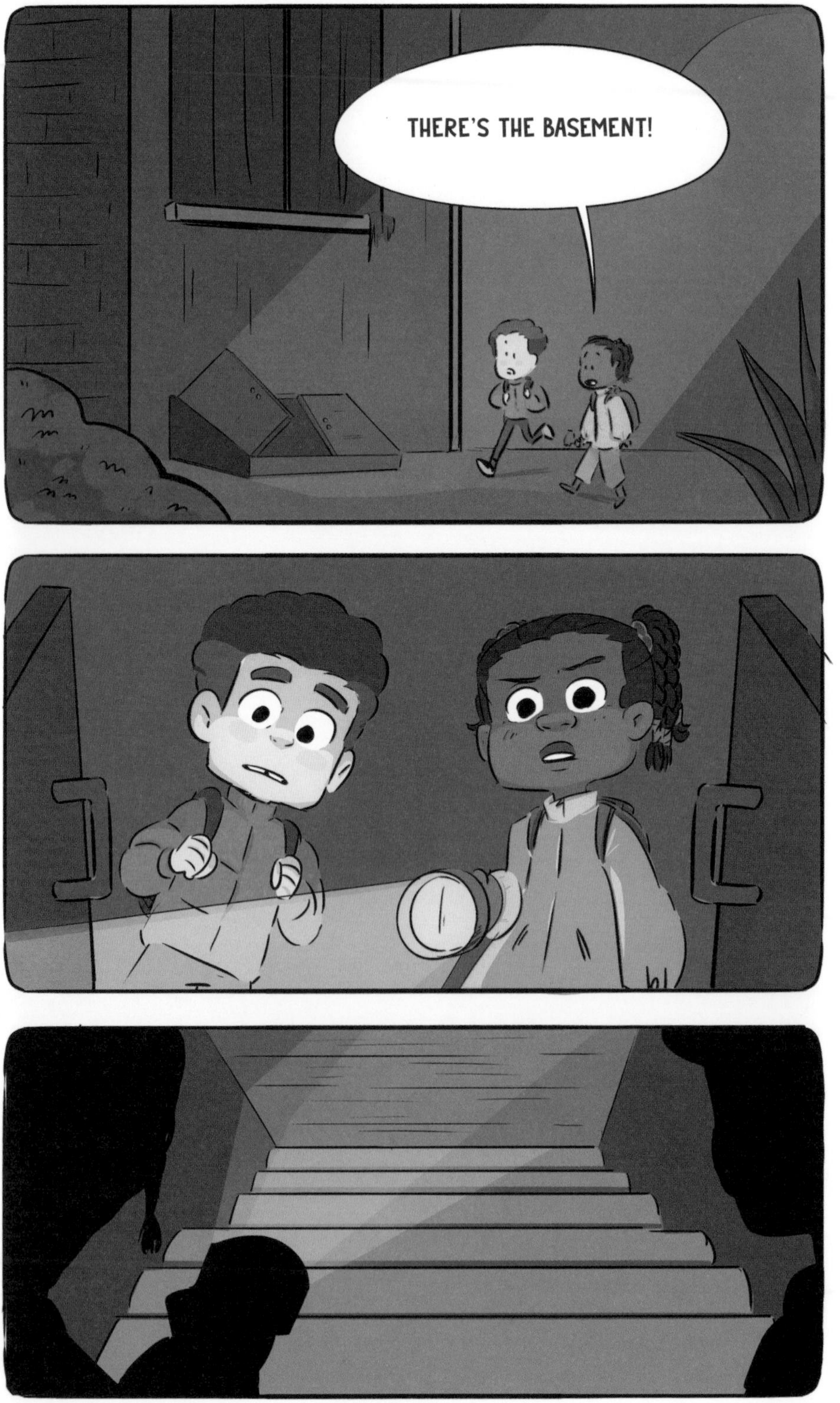
THERE'S THE BASEMENT!

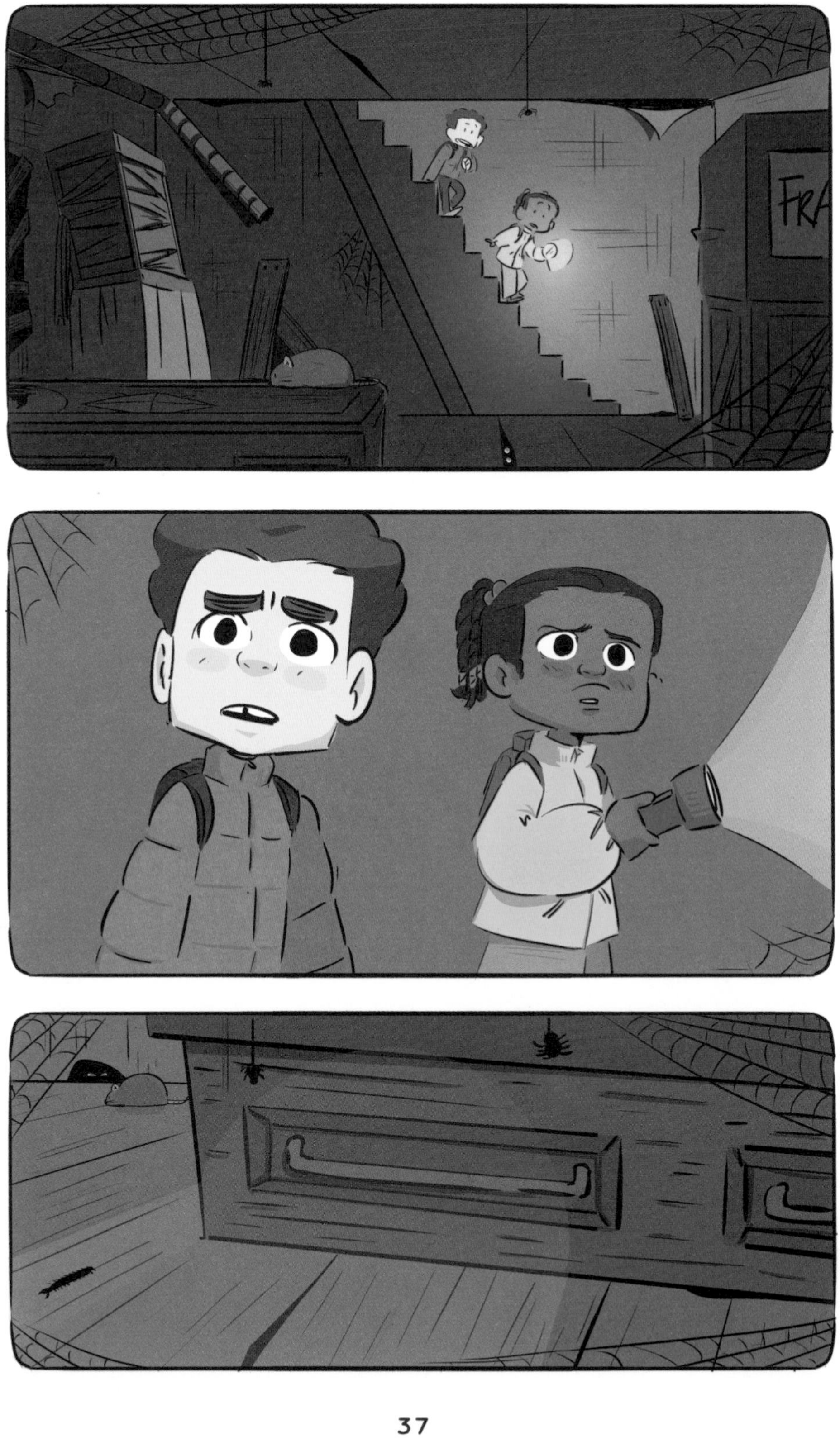
FRA

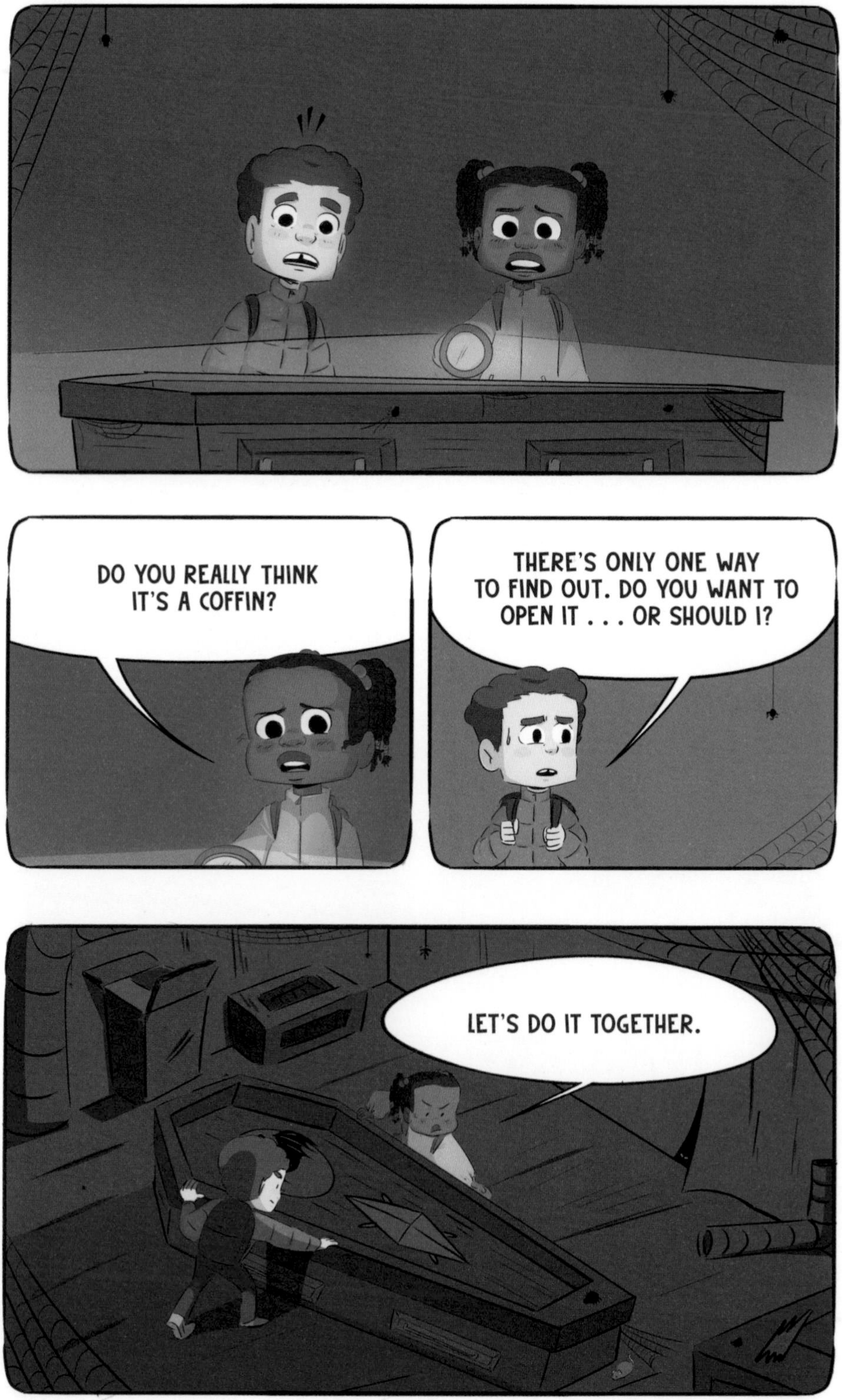
DO YOU REALLY THINK IT'S A COFFIN?
THERE'S ONLY ONE WAY TO FIND OUT. DO YOU WANT TO OPEN IT . . . OR SHOULD I?
LET'S DO IT TOGETHER.

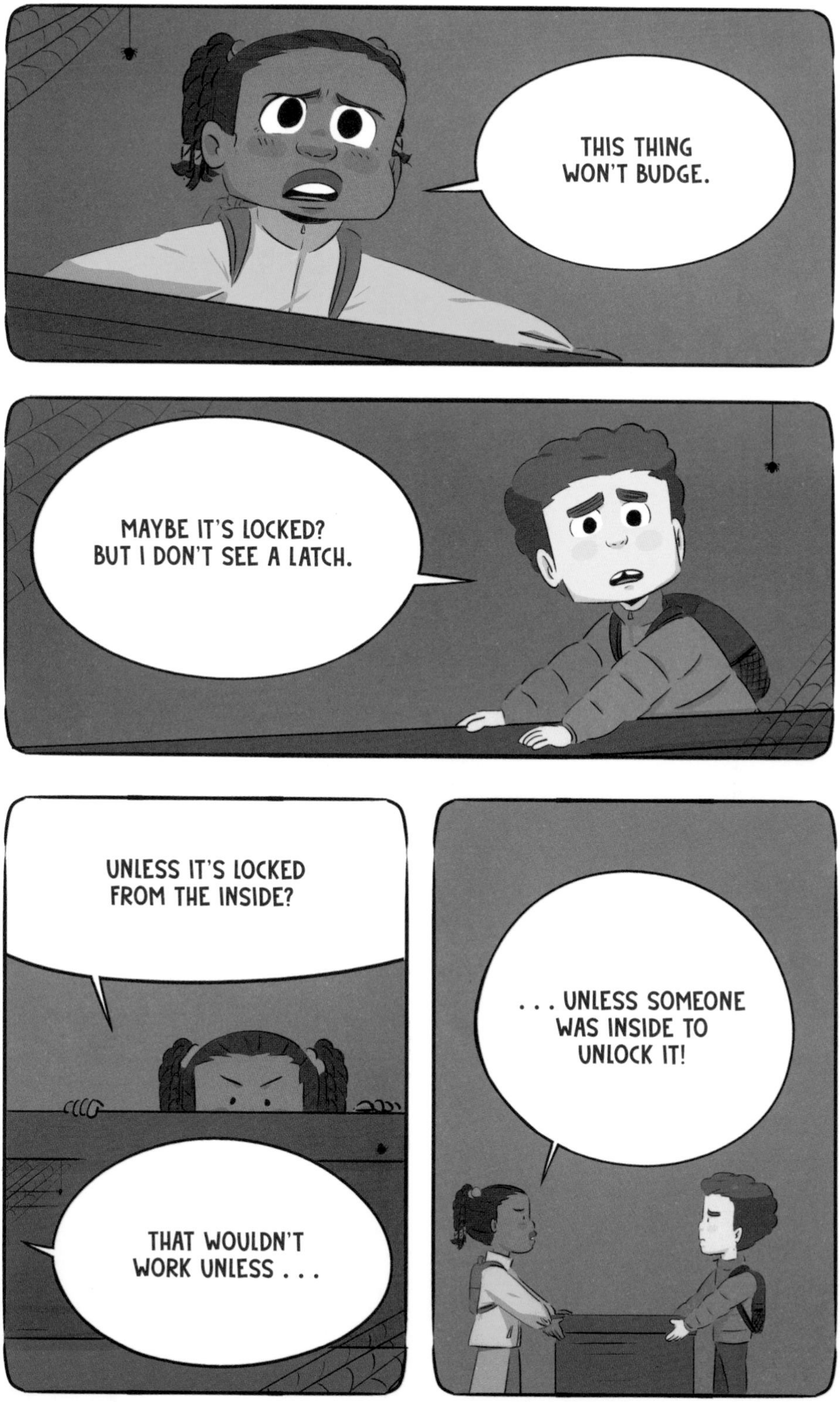
THIS THING WON'T BUDGE.
MAYBE IT'S LOCKED? BUT I DON'T SEE A LATCH.
UNLESS IT'S LOCKED FROM THE INSIDE?
THAT WOULDN'T WORK UNLESS . . .
. . . UNLESS SOMEONE WAS INSIDE TO UNLOCK IT!

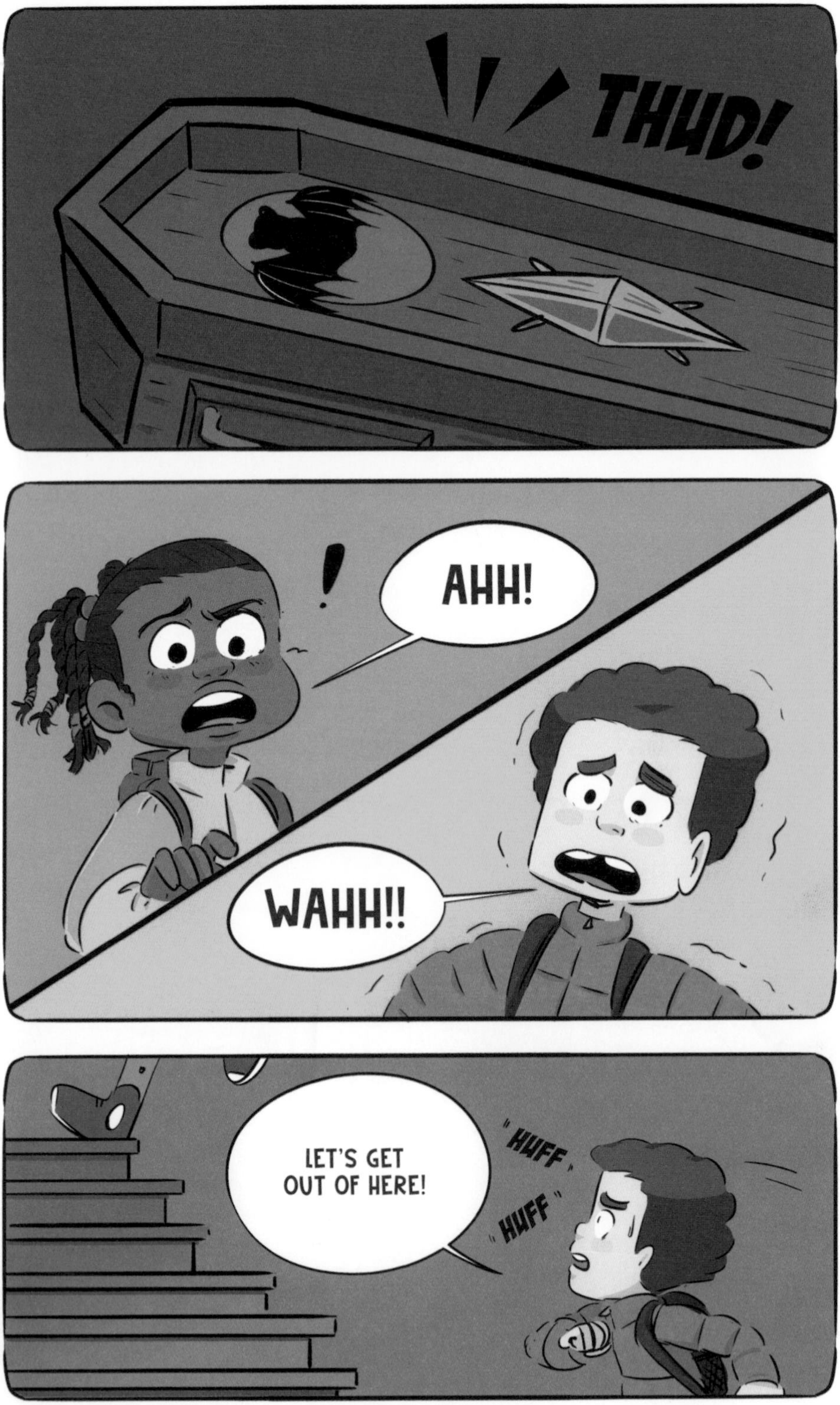
THUD!
!
AHH!
WAHH!!
LET'S GET OUT OF HERE!
HUFF
HUFF

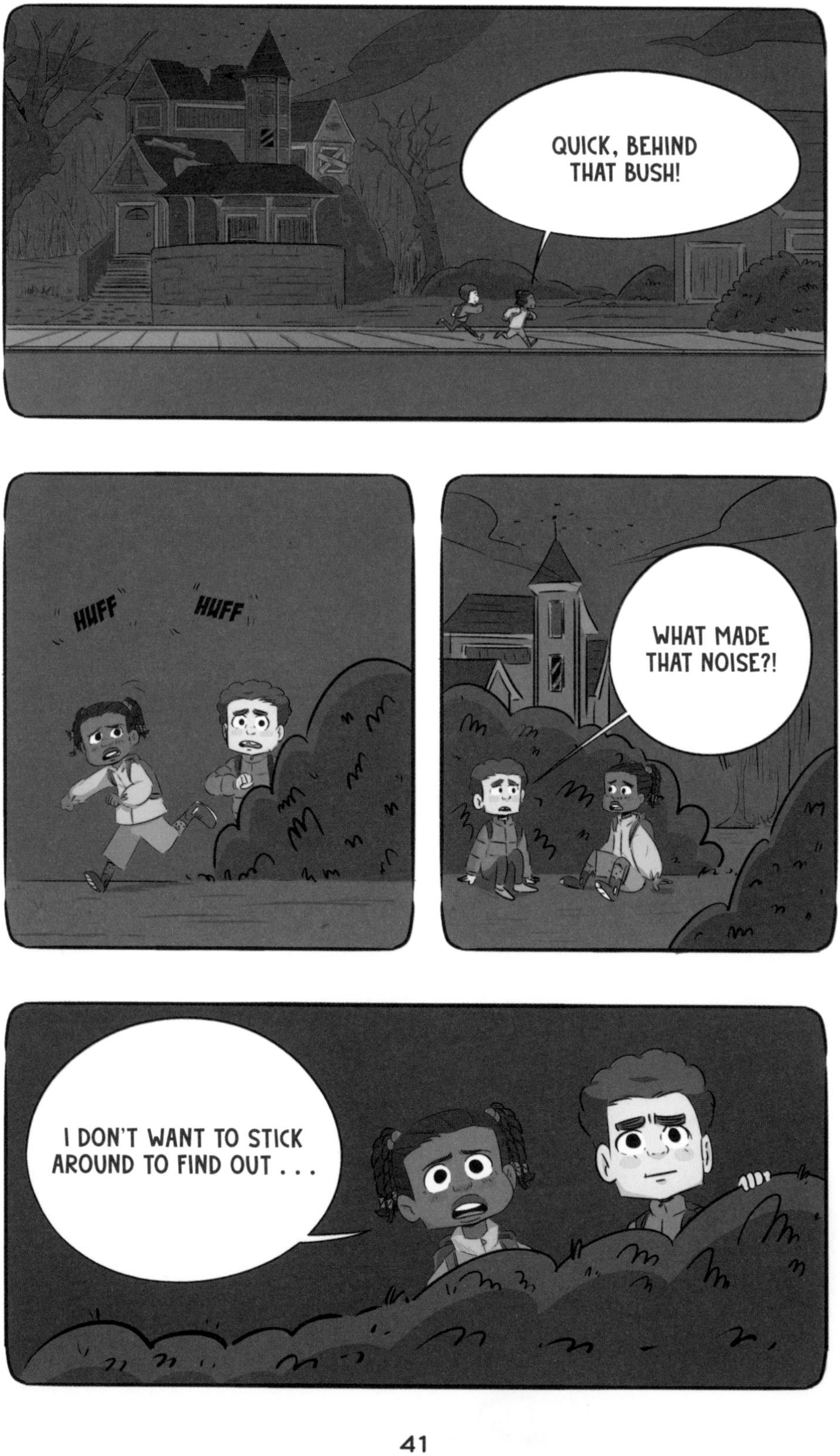
QUICK, BEHIND THAT BUSH!
HUFF
HUFF
WHAT MADE THAT NOISE?!
I DON'T WANT TO STICK AROUND TO FIND OUT . . .

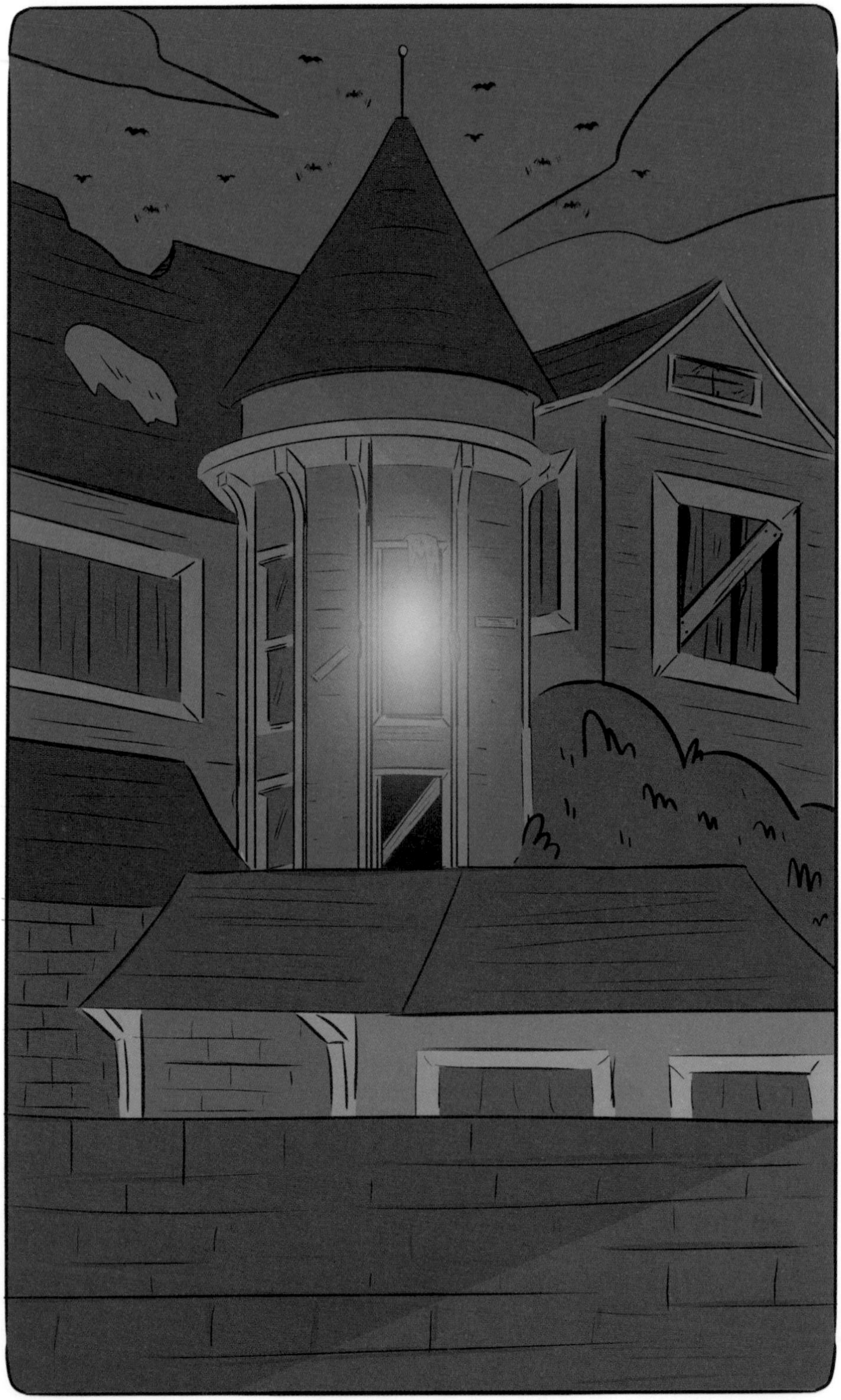

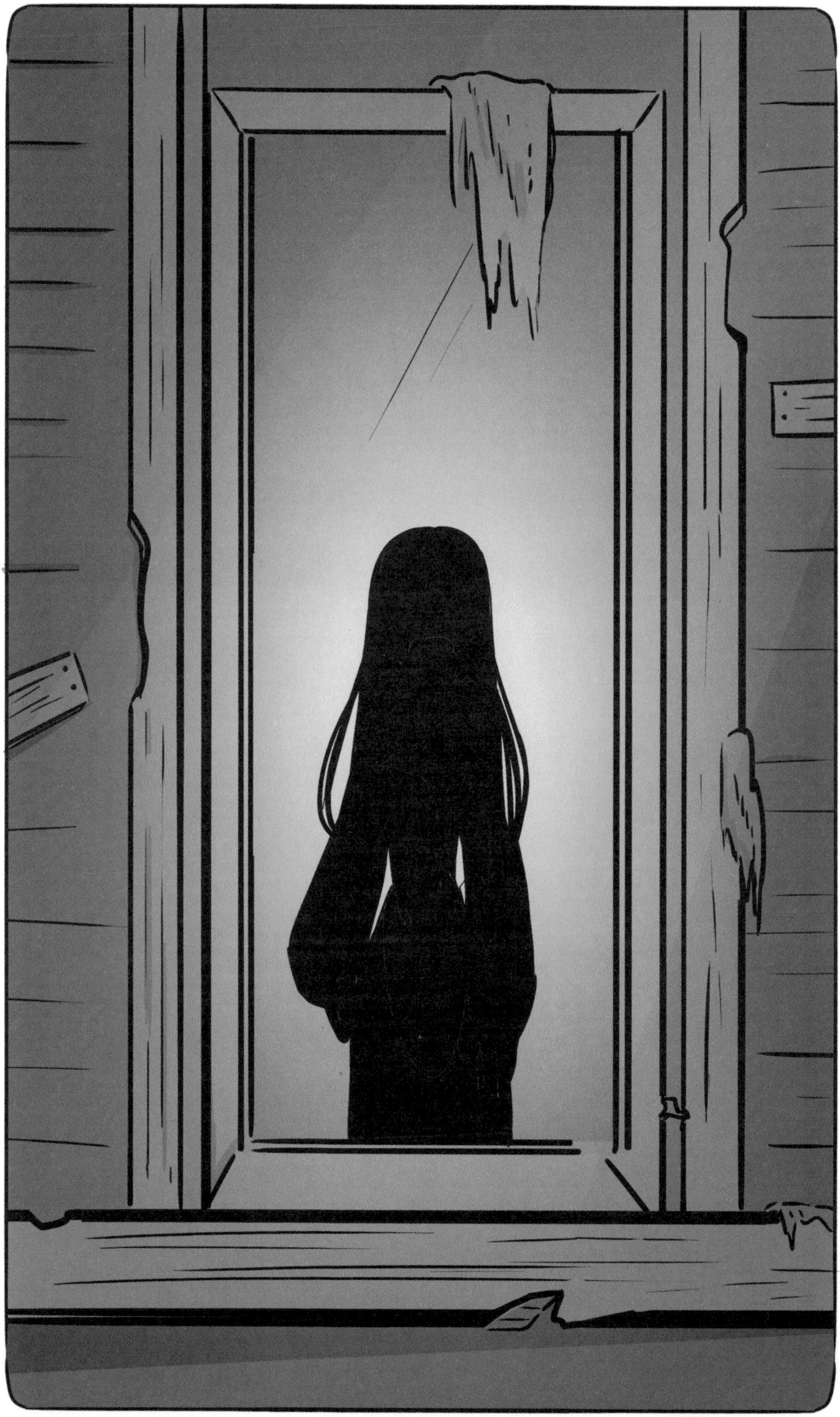

CHAPTER 4 HYPNOTIZED

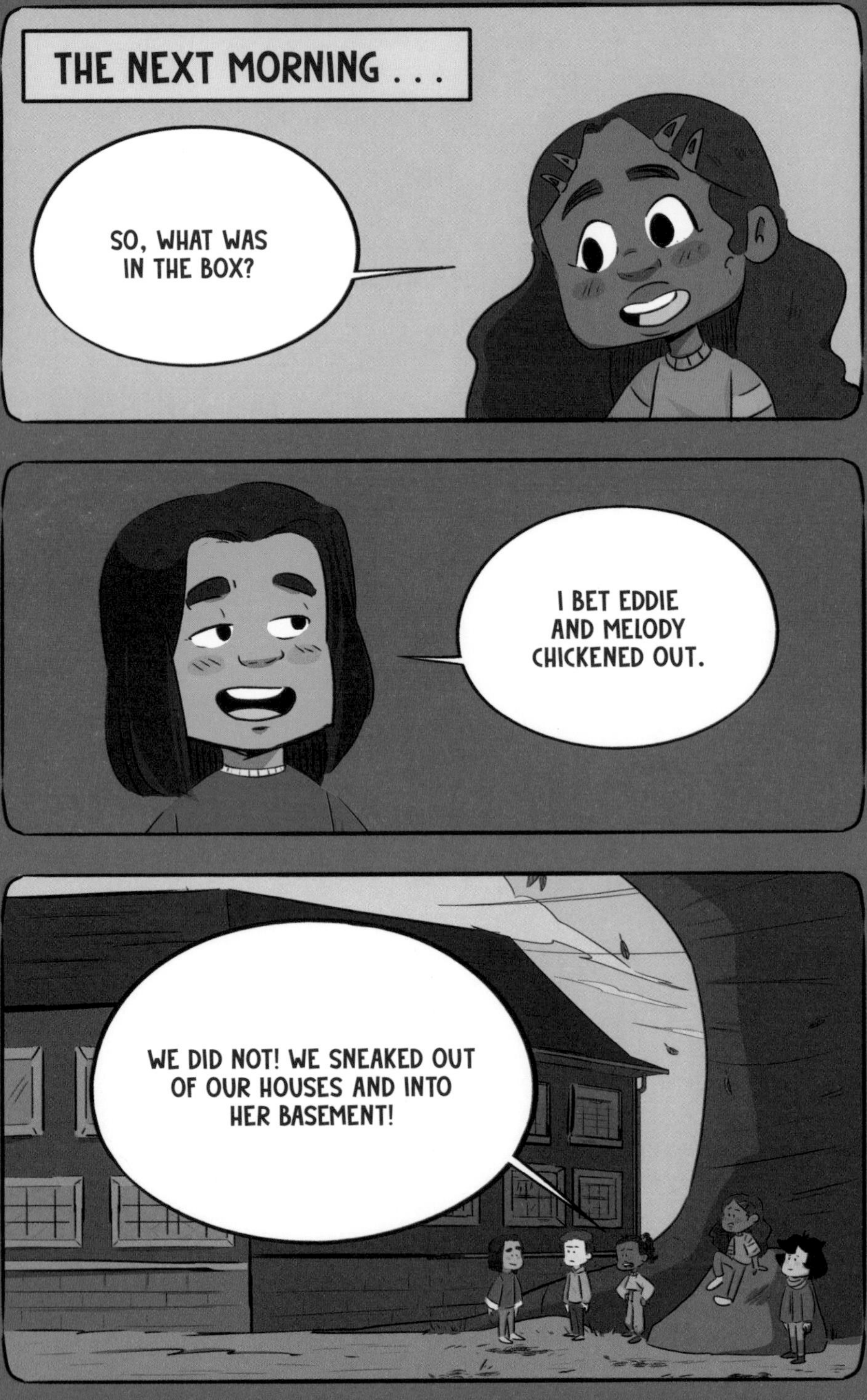
THE NEXT MORNING . . .
SO, WHAT WAS IN THE BOX?
I BET EDDIE AND MELODY CHICKENED OUT.
WE DID NOT! WE SNEAKED OUT OF OUR HOUSES AND INTO HER BASEMENT!

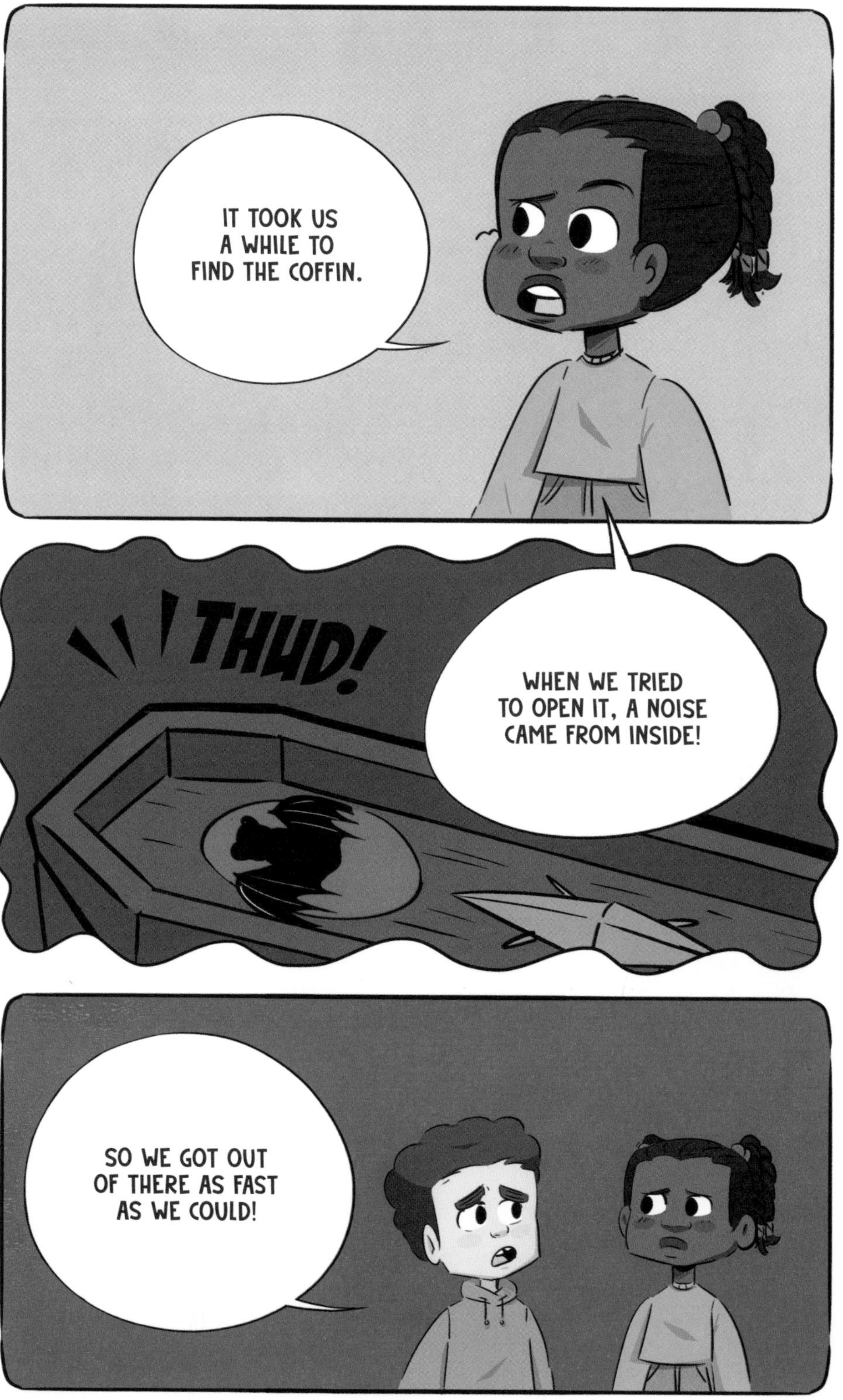
IT TOOK US A WHILE TO FIND THE COFFIN.
THUD!
WHEN WE TRIED TO OPEN IT, A NOISE CAME FROM INSIDE!
SO WE GOT OUT OF THERE AS FAST AS WE COULD!

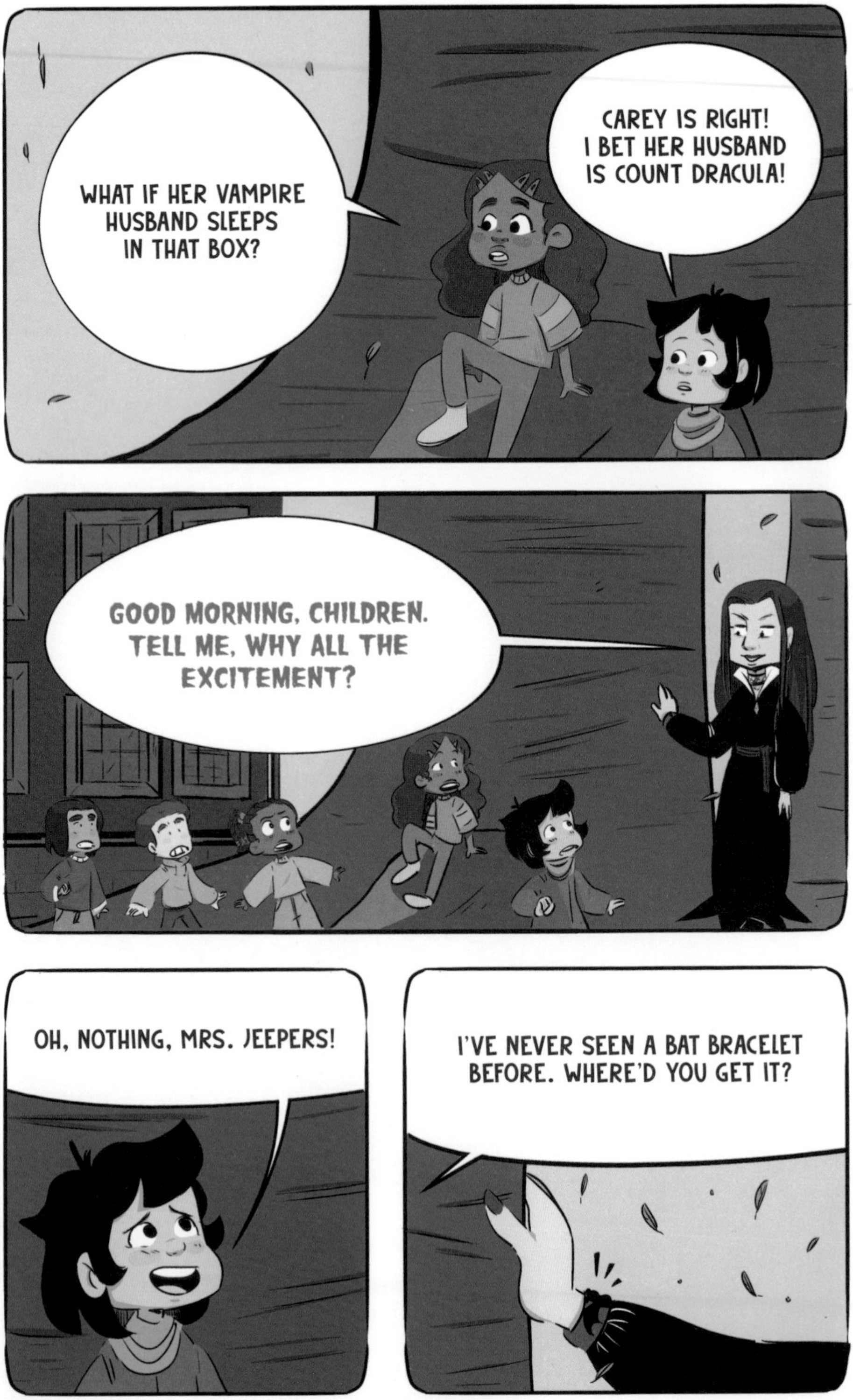
WHAT IF HER VAMPIRE HUSBAND SLEEPS IN THAT BOX?
CAREY IS RIGHT! I BET HER HUSBAND IS COUNT DRACULA!
GOOD MORNING, CHILDREN. TELL ME, WHY ALL THE EXCITEMENT?
OH, NOTHING, MRS. JEEPERS!
I'VE NEVER SEEN A BAT BRACELET BEFORE. WHERE'D YOU GET IT?

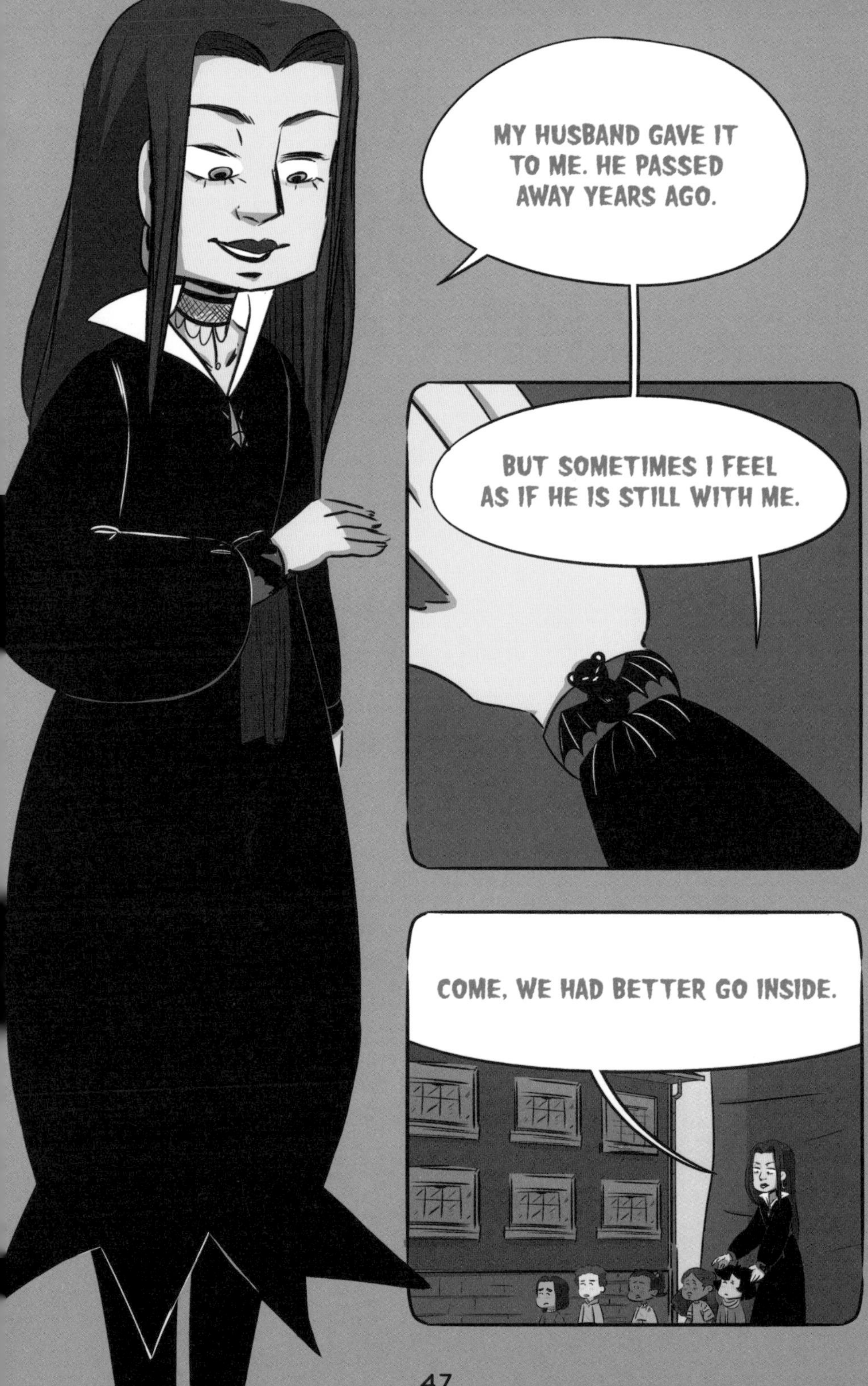
MY HUSBAND GAVE IT TO ME. HE PASSED AWAY YEARS AGO.
BUT SOMETIMES I FEEL AS IF HE IS STILL WITH ME.
COME, WE HAD BETTER GO INSIDE.

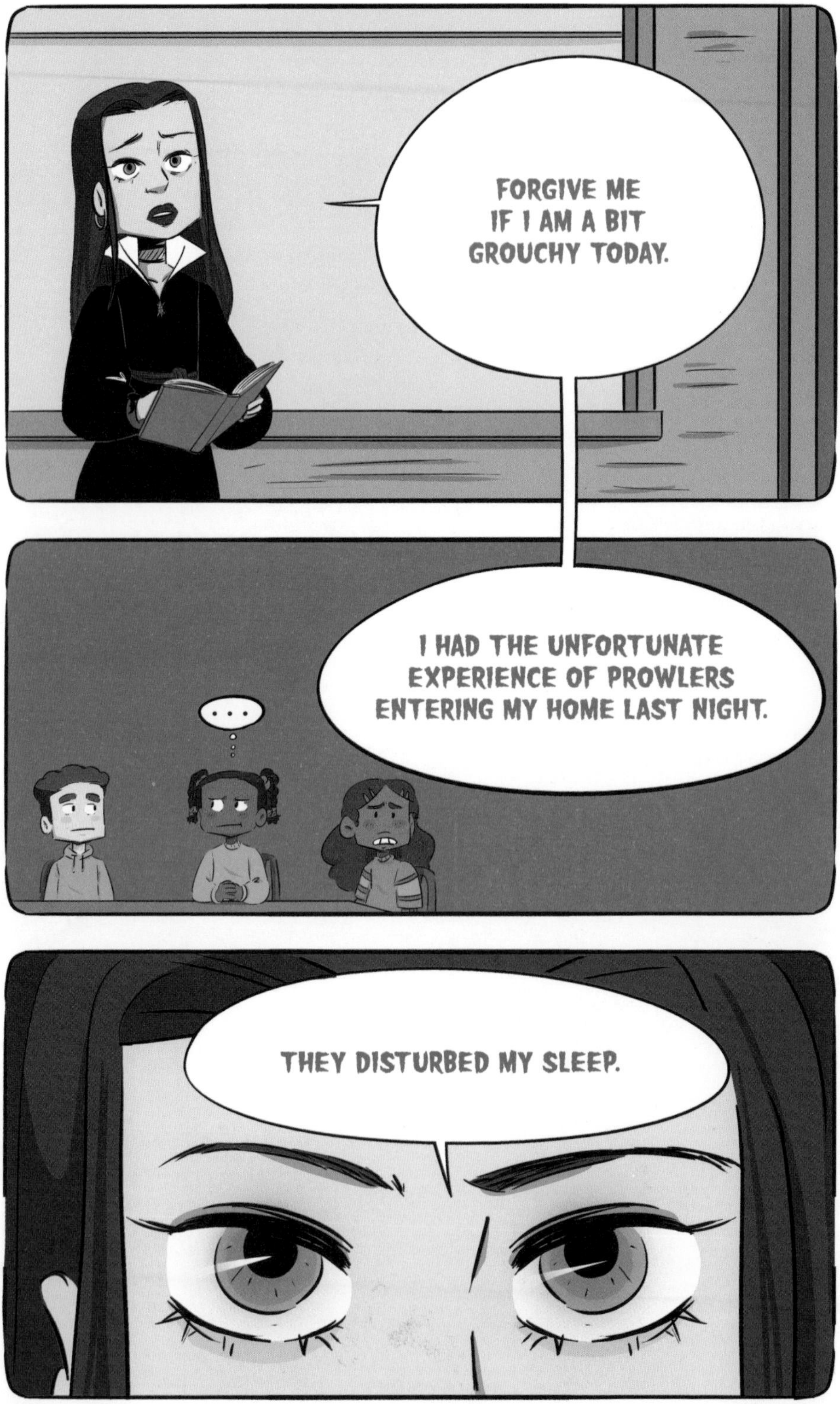
FORGIVE ME IF I AM A BIT GROUCHY TODAY.
...
I HAD THE UNFORTUNATE EXPERIENCE OF PROWLERS ENTERING MY HOME LAST NIGHT.
THEY DISTURBED MY SLEEP.

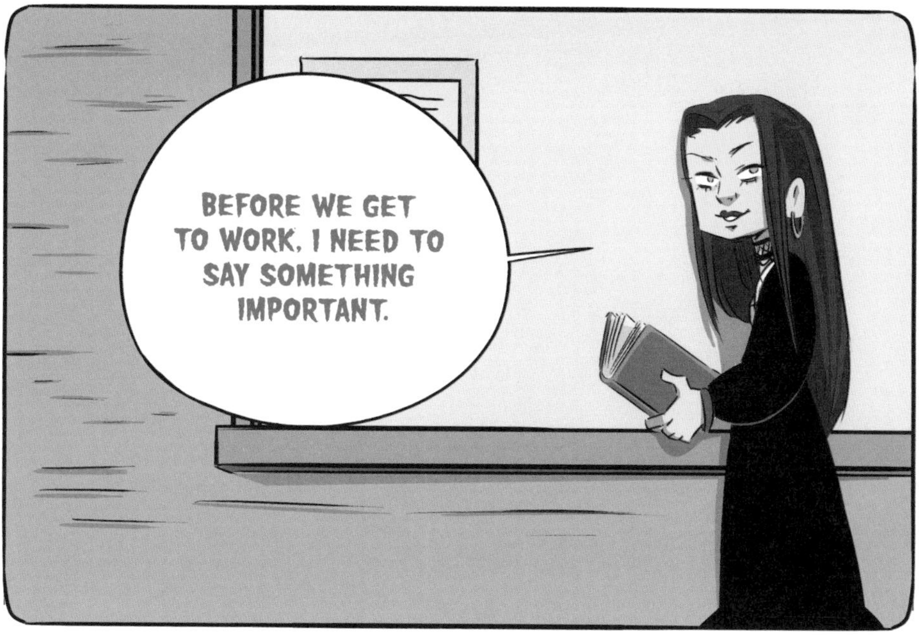
BEFORE WE GET TO WORK, I NEED TO SAY SOMETHING IMPORTANT.

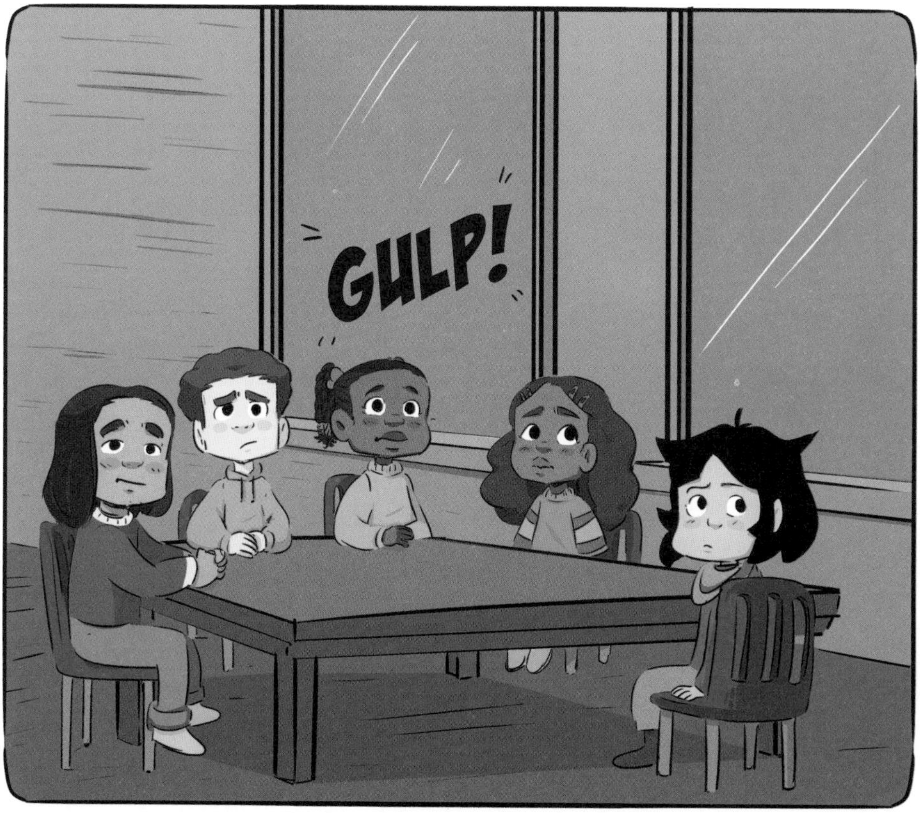
GULP!

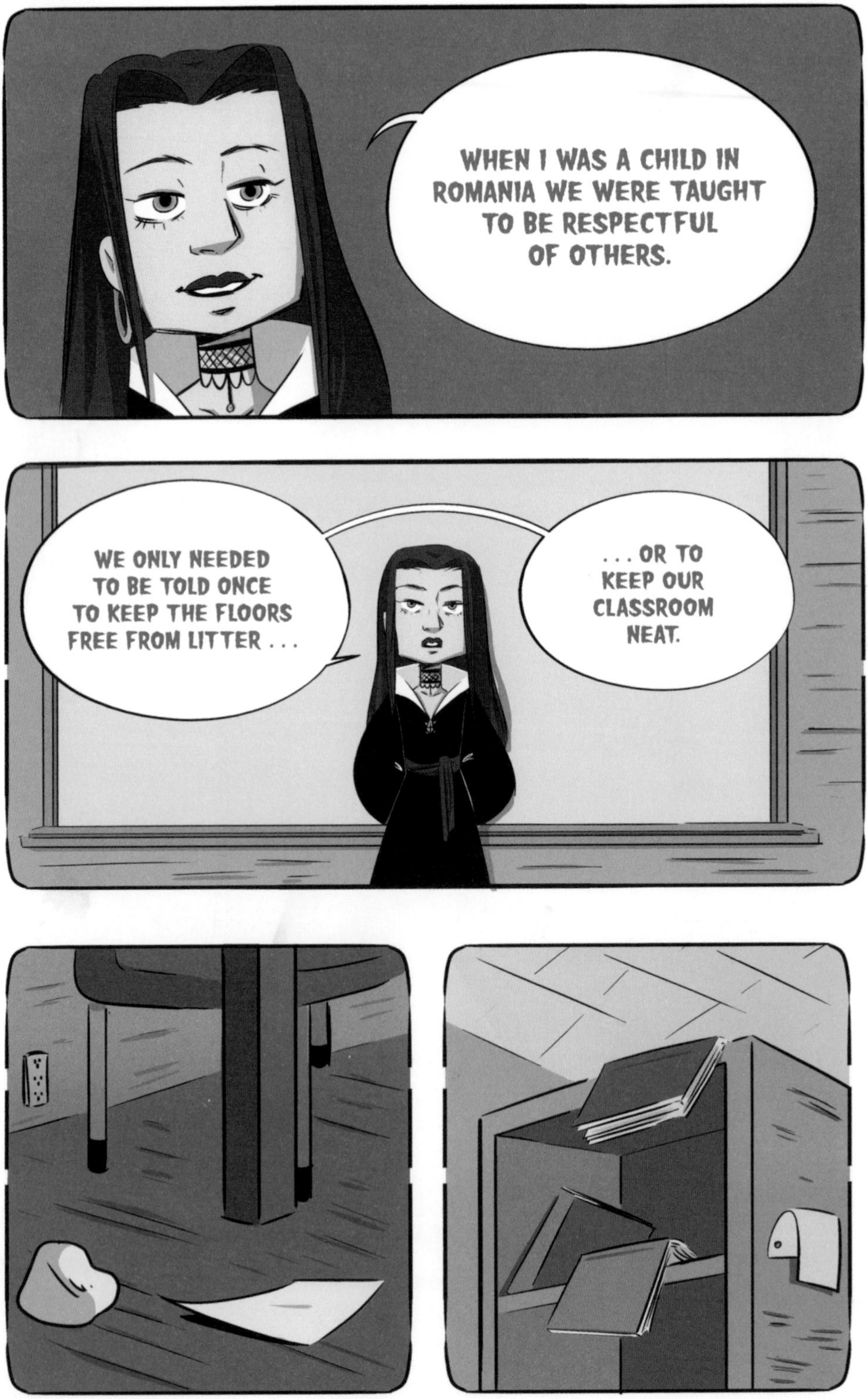
WHEN I WAS A CHILD IN ROMANIA WE WERE TAUGHT TO BE RESPECTFUL OF OTHERS.
WE ONLY NEEDED TO BE TOLD ONCE TO KEEP THE FLOORS FREE FROM LITTER . . .
. . . OR TO KEEP OUR CLASSROOM NEAT.

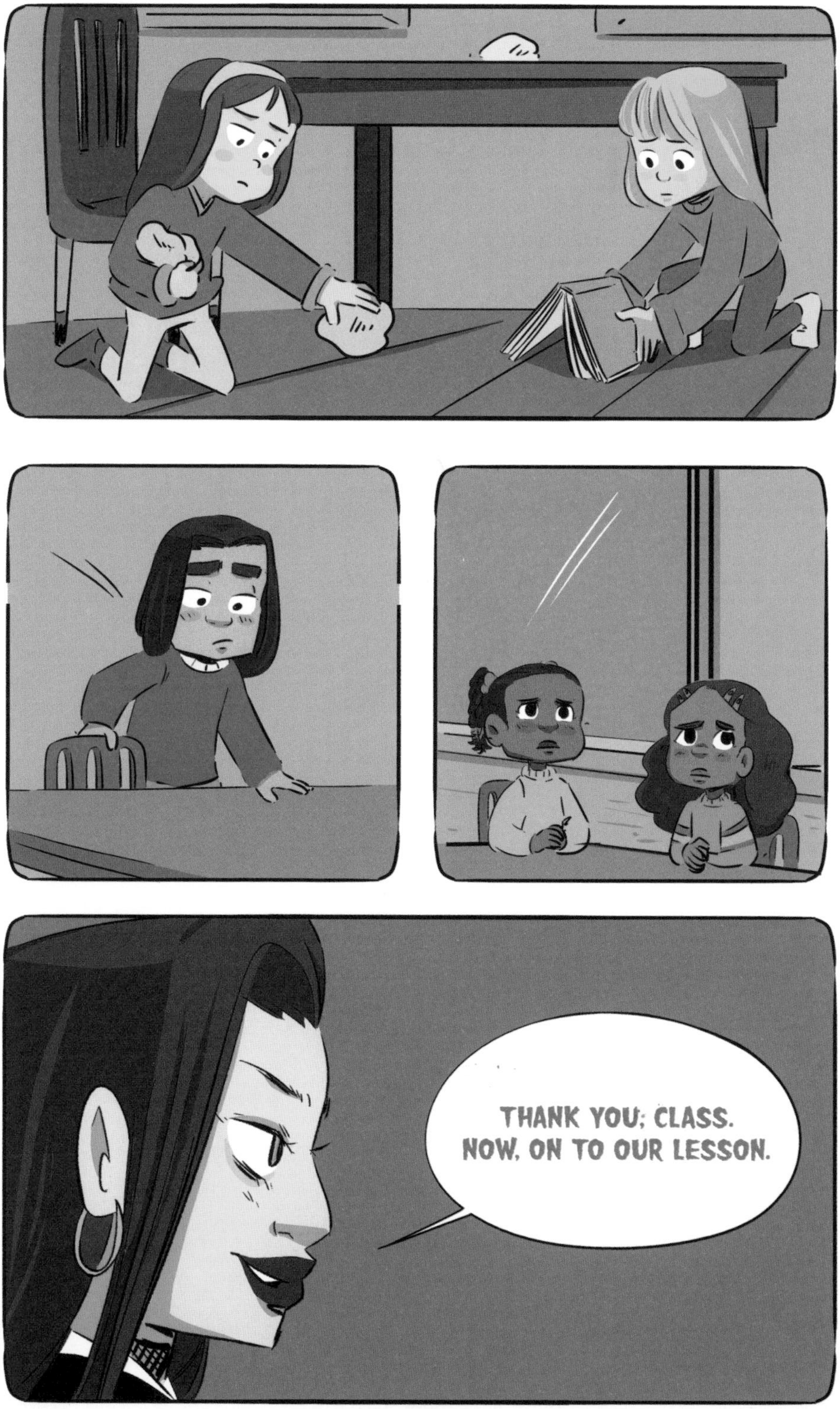
THANK YOU; CLASS.
NOW, ON TO OUR LESSON.

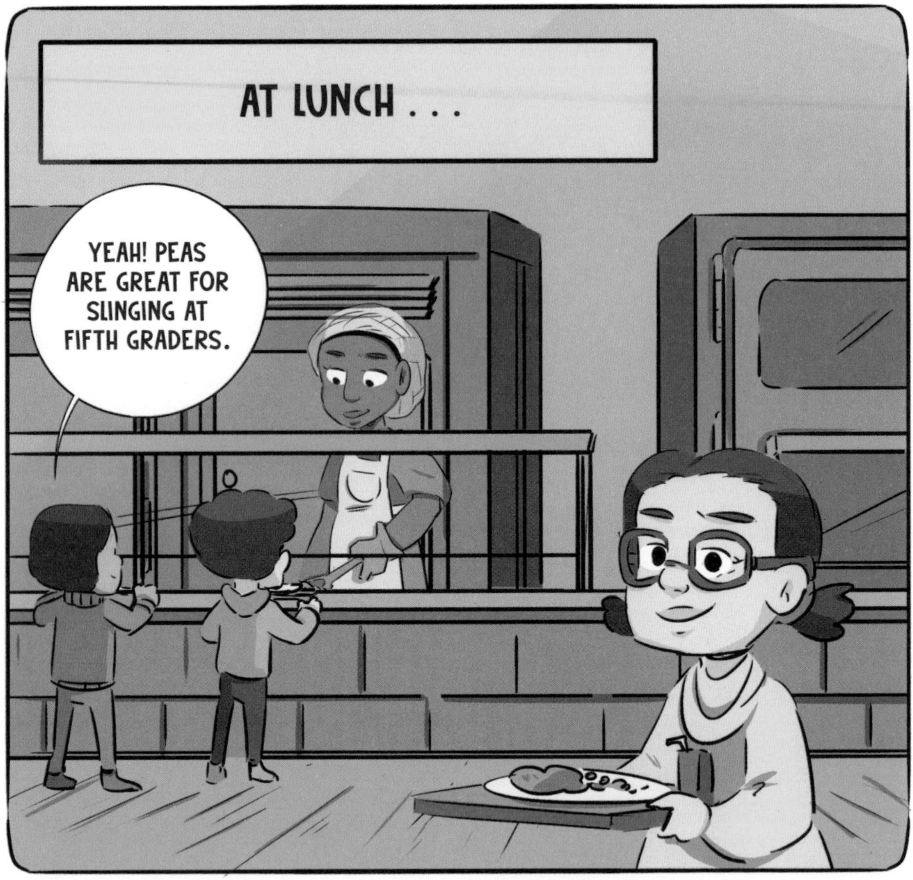
AT LUNCH . . .
YEAH! PEAS ARE GREAT FOR SLINGING AT FIFTH GRADERS.

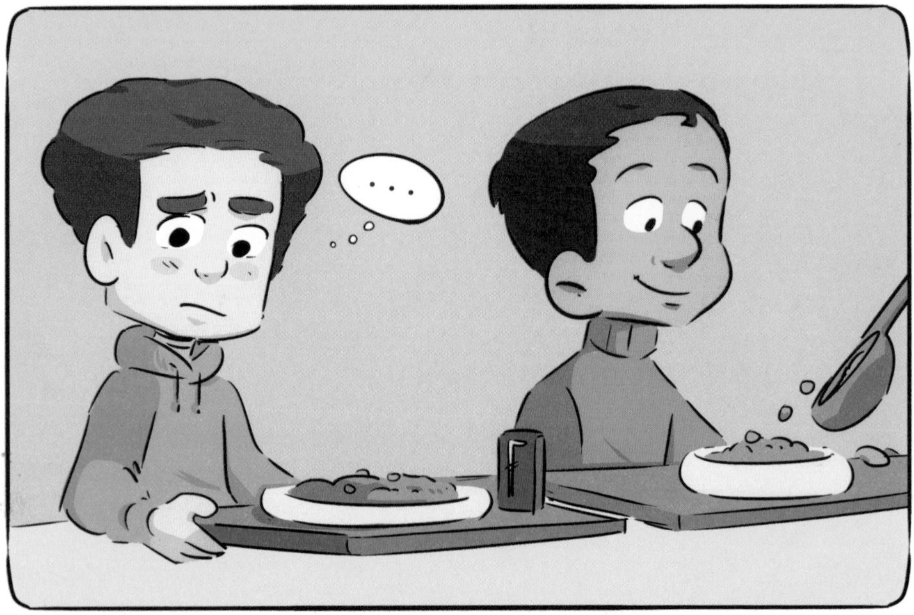
. . .

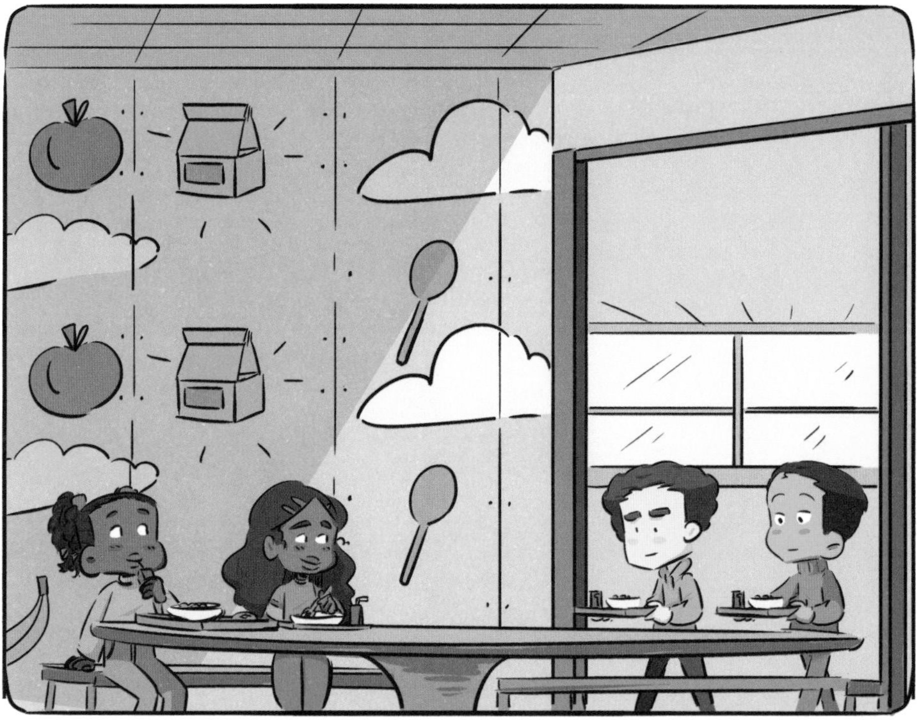

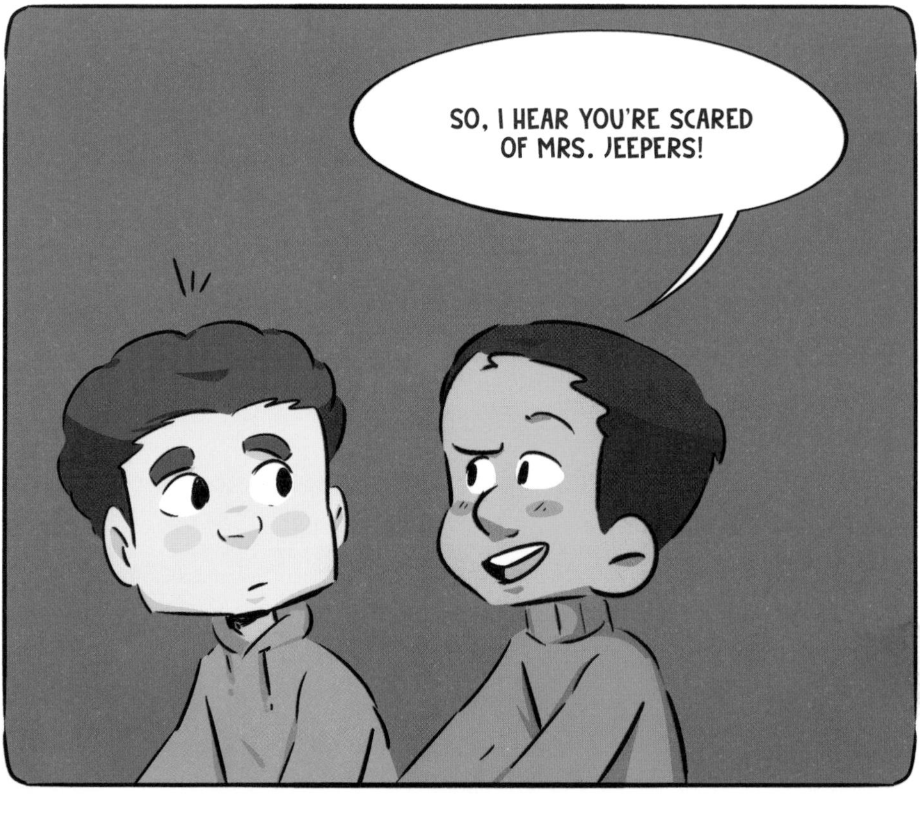
SO, I HEAR YOU'RE SCARED OF MRS. JEEPERS!

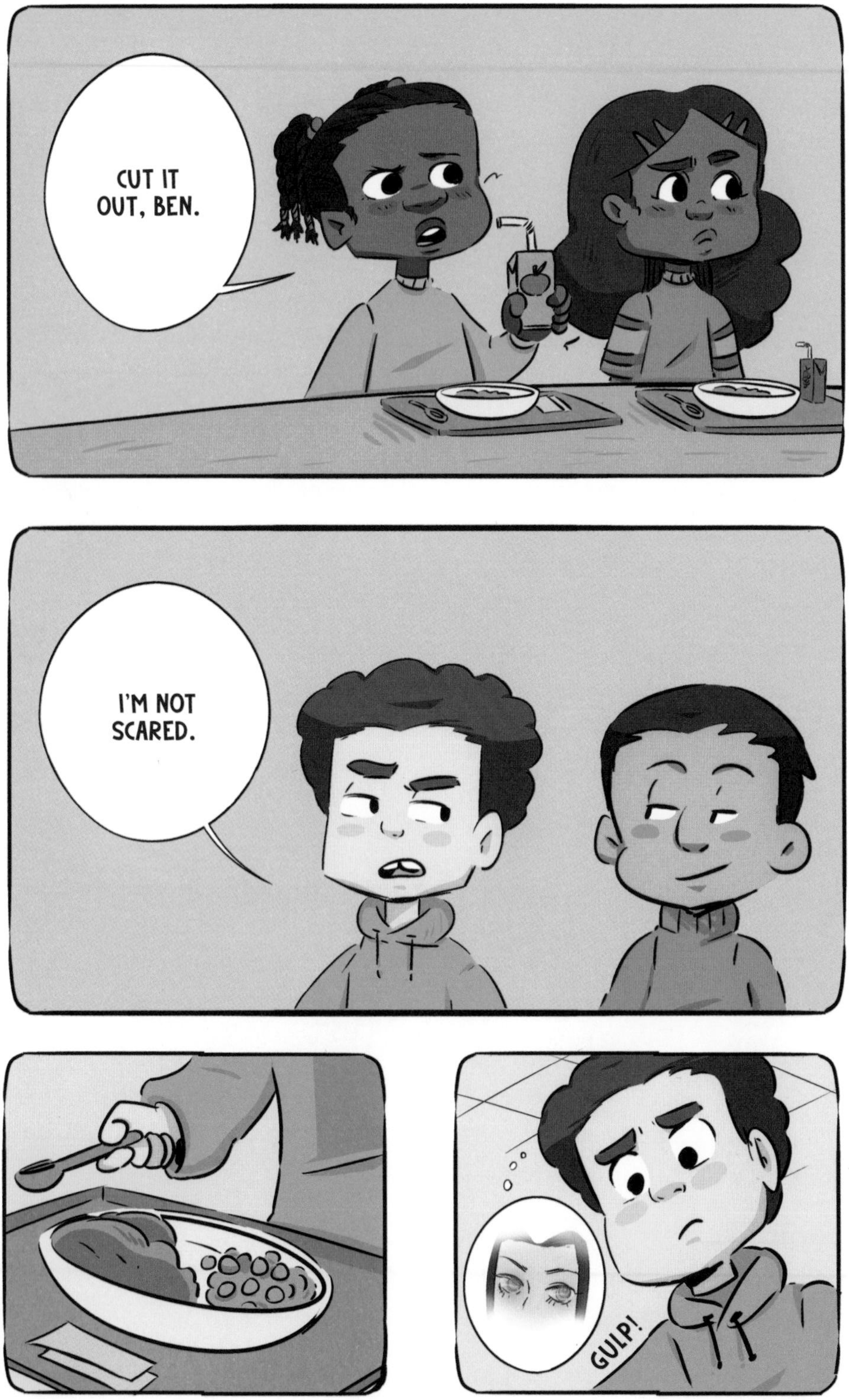
CUT IT OUT, BEN.
I'M NOT SCARED.
GULP!

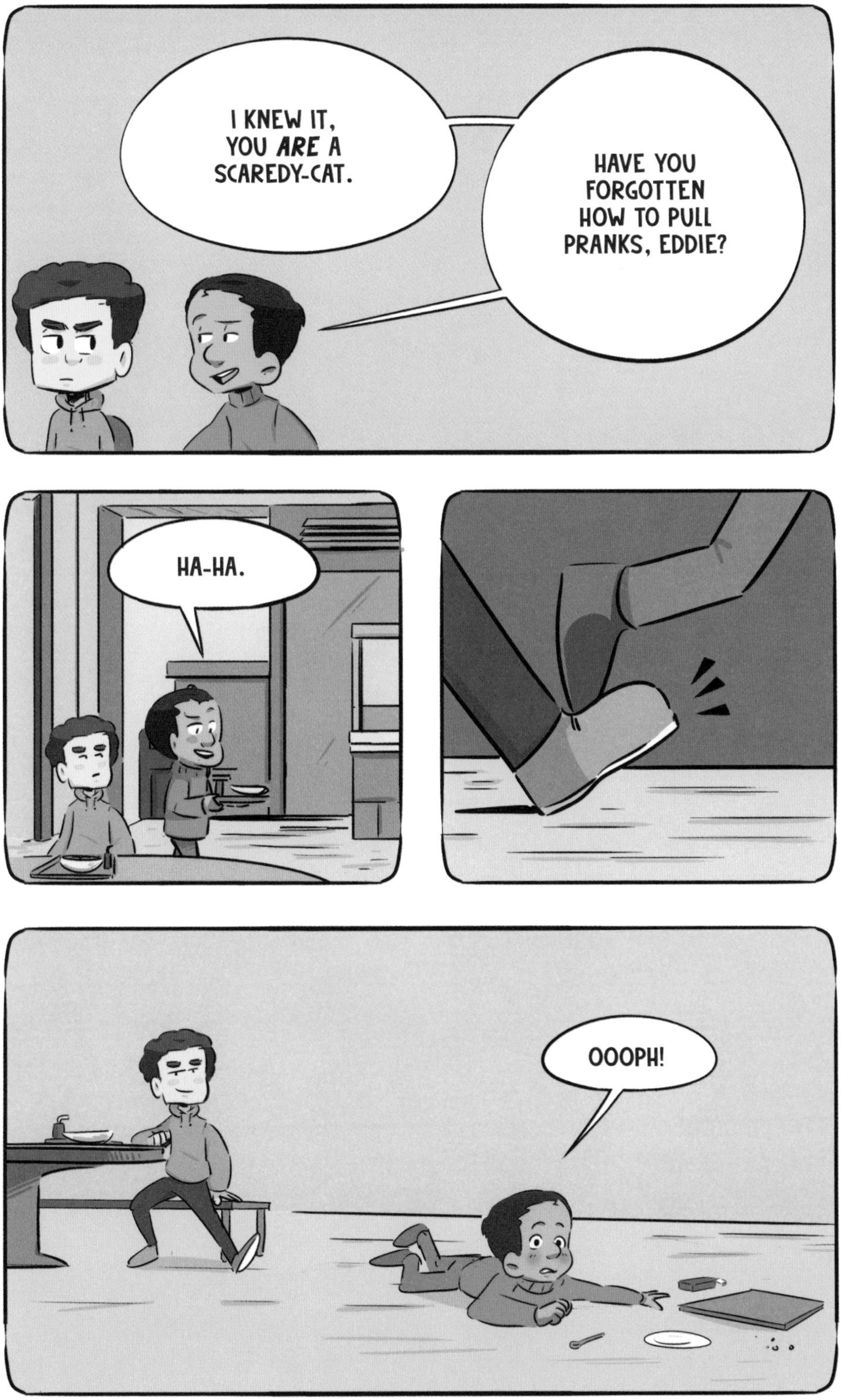
I KNEW IT, YOU ARE A SCAREDY-CAT.
HAVE YOU FORGOTTEN HOW TO PULL PRANKS, EDDIE?
HA-HA.
OOOPH!

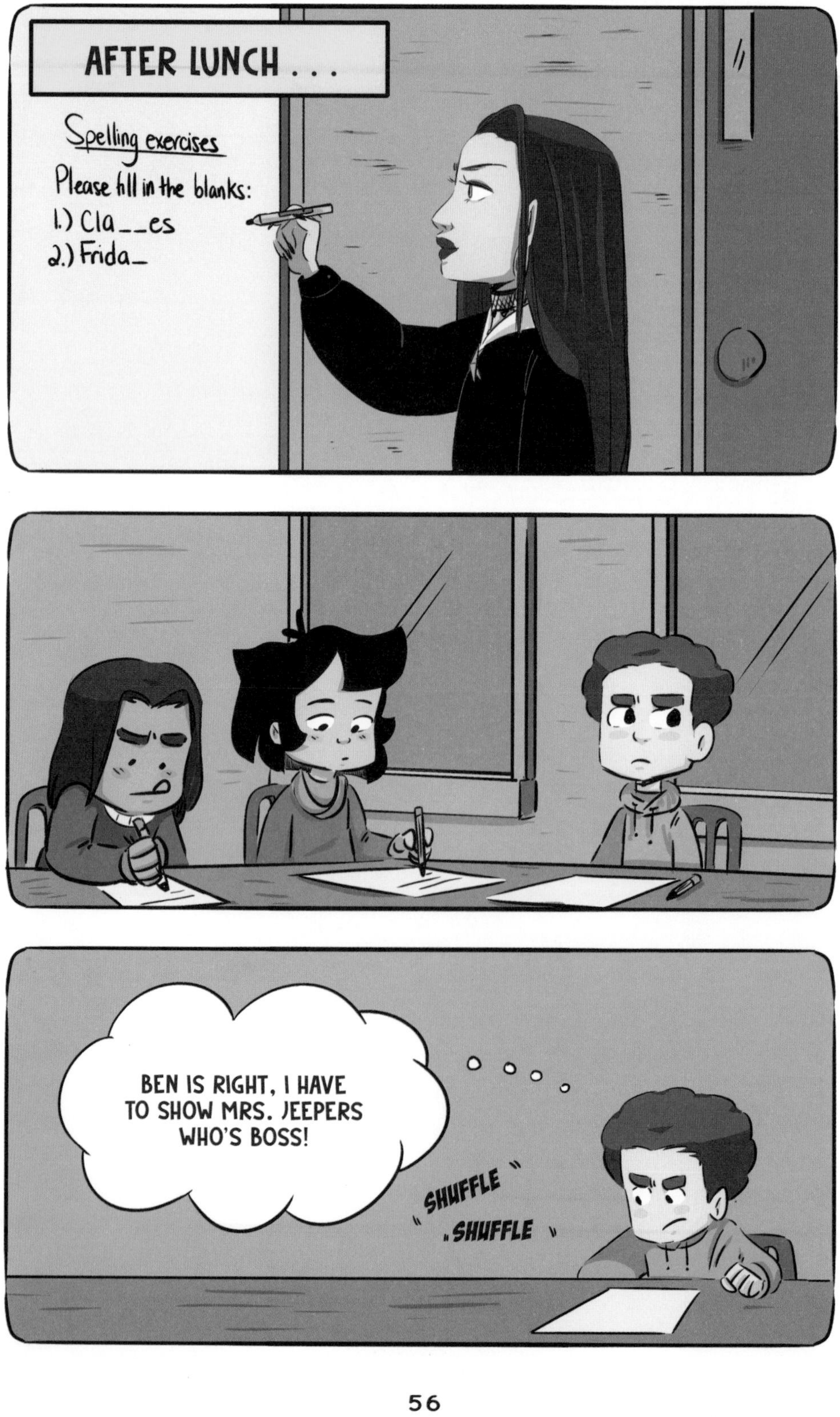
AFTER LUNCH . . .
Spelling exercises
Please fill in the blanks:
1.) Cla__es
2.) Frida_
BEN IS RIGHT, I HAVE TO SHOW MRS. JEEPERS WHO'S BOSS!
"SHUFFLE"
"SHUFFLE"

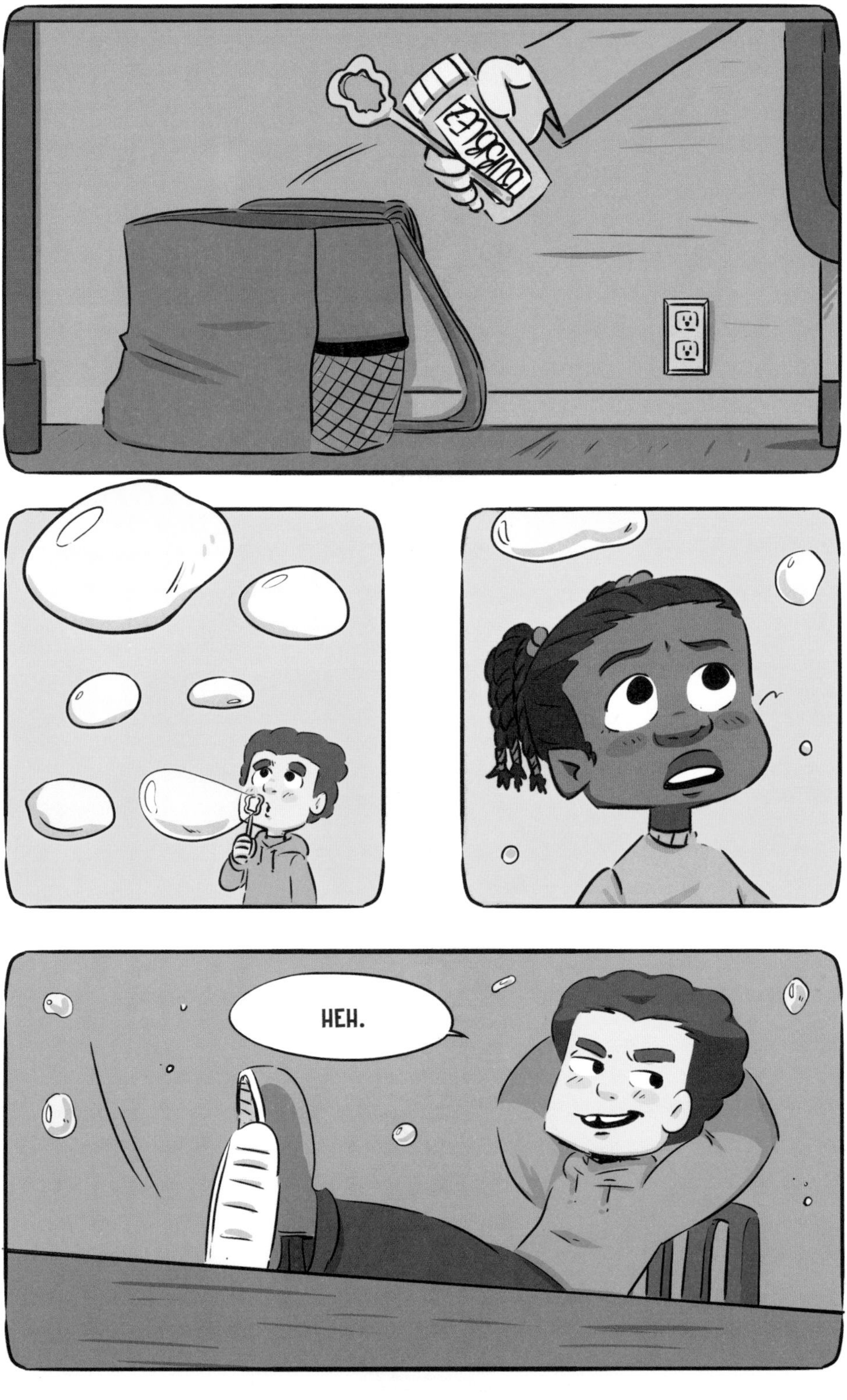
BUBBLEZ
HEH.

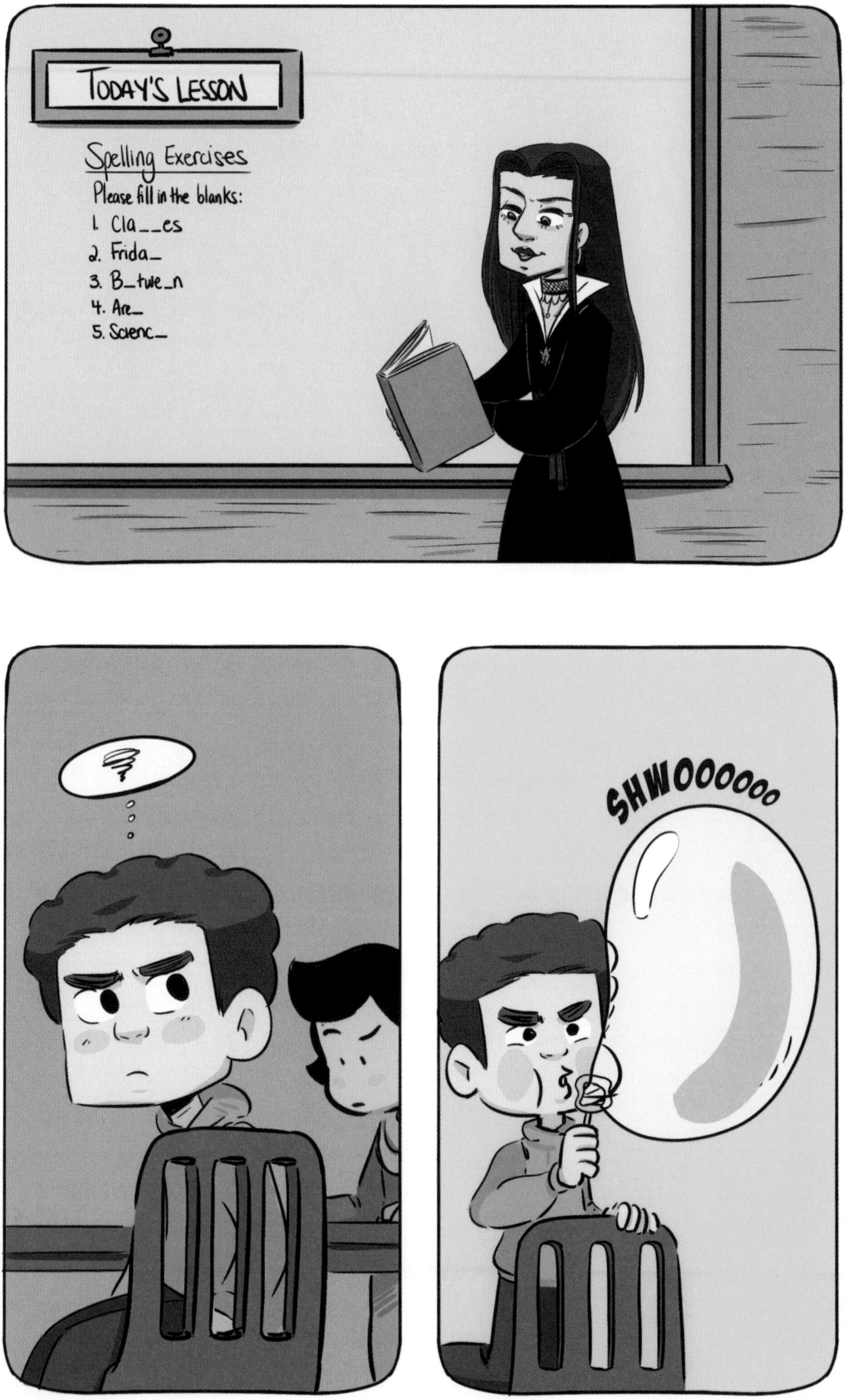
TODAY'S LESSON
Spelling Exercises
Please fill in the blanks:
1. Cla__es
2. Frida_
3. B_twe_n
4. Are_
5. Scienc_
SHWOOOOOO

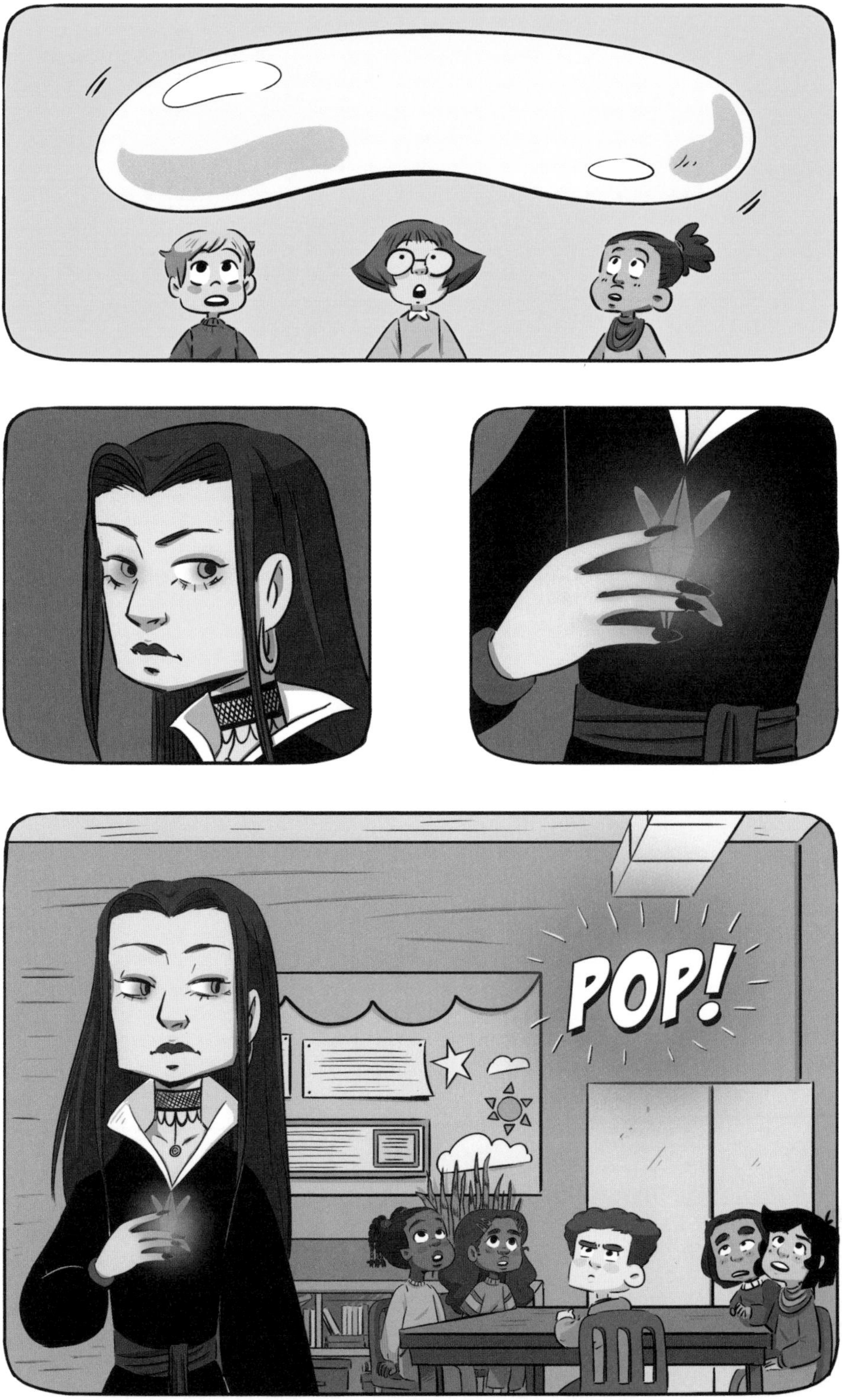
POP!

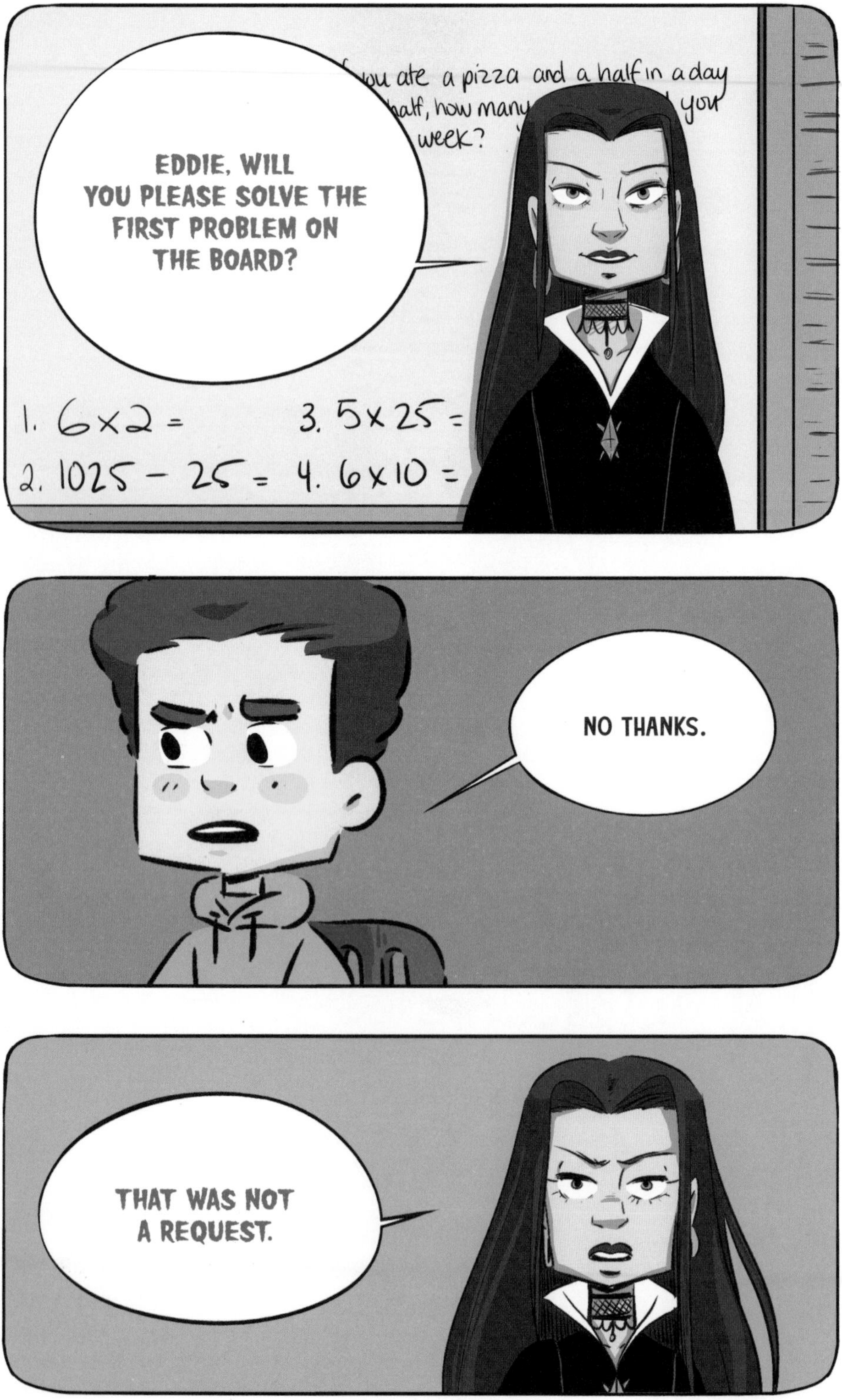
EDDIE, WILL YOU PLEASE SOLVE THE FIRST PROBLEM ON THE BOARD?
1. 6x2 =
3. 5x25 =
2. 1025 - 25 =
4. 6x10 =
NO THANKS.
THAT WAS NOT A REQUEST.

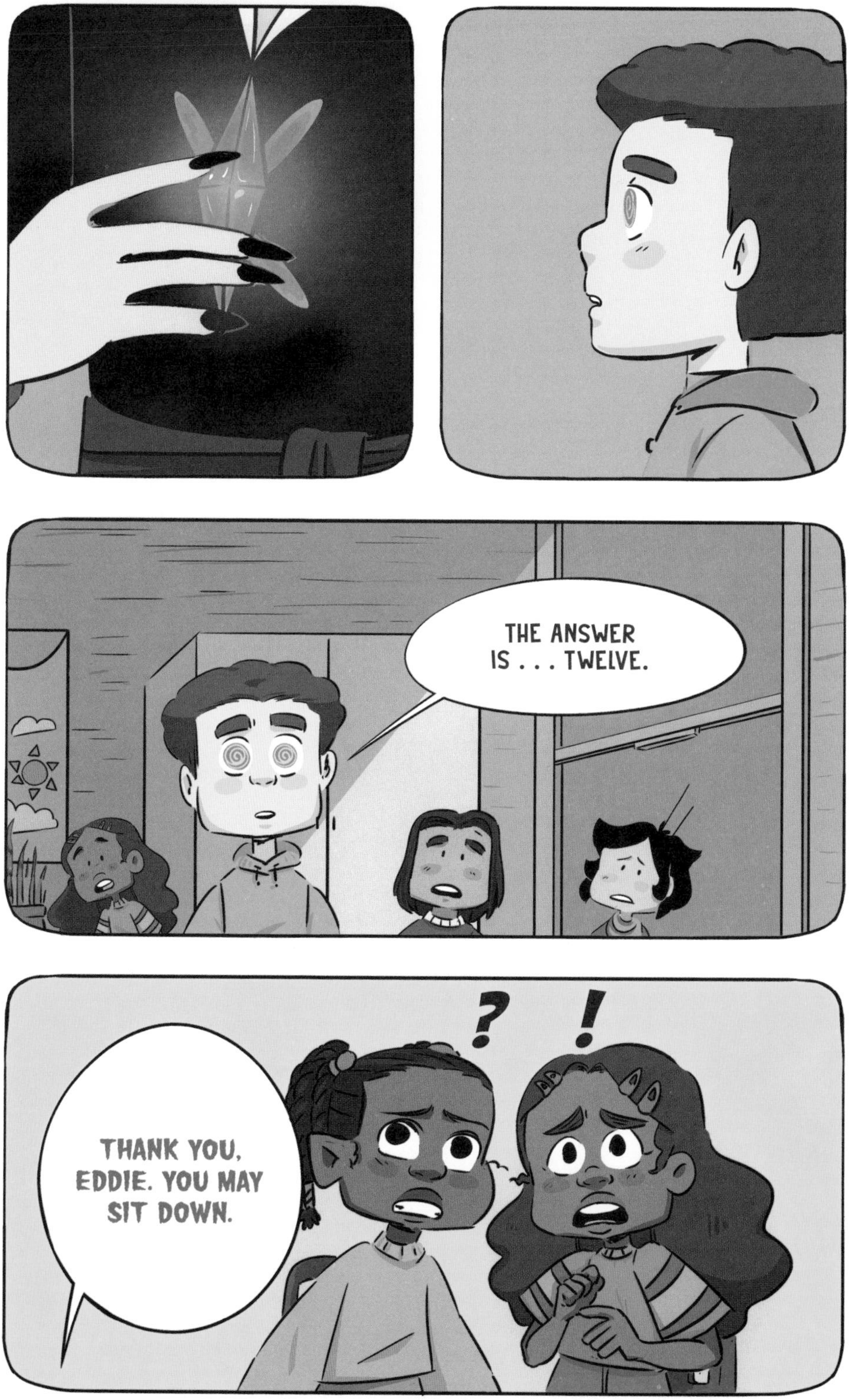
THE ANSWER IS . . . TWELVE.
?
!
THANK YOU, EDDIE. YOU MAY SIT DOWN.

CHAPTER 5 NO ORDINARY TEACHER

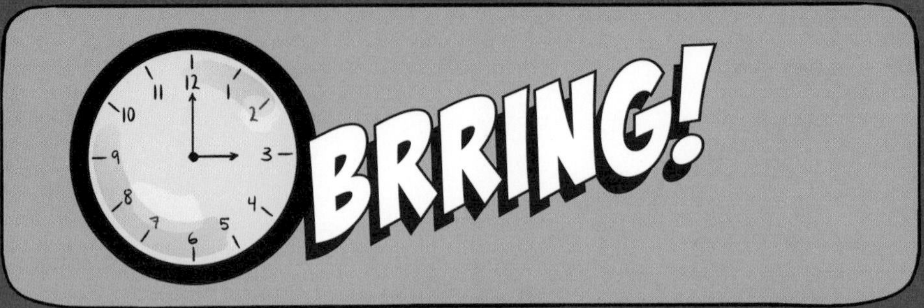
BRRING!

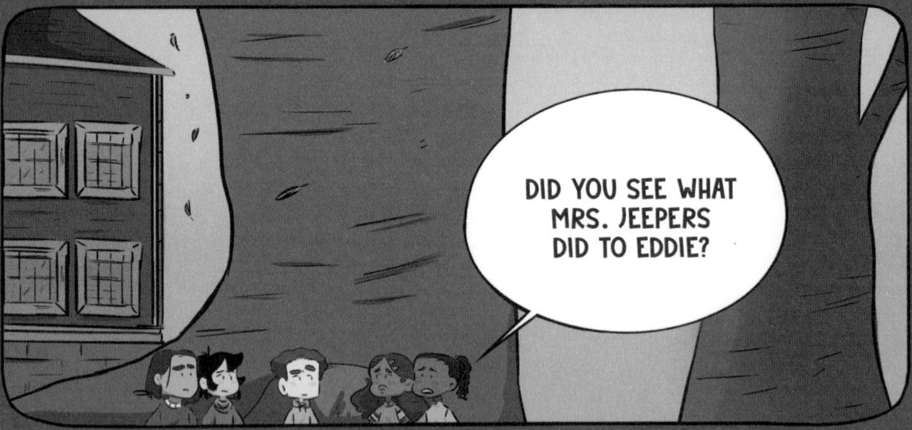
DID YOU SEE WHAT MRS. JEEPERS DID TO EDDIE?

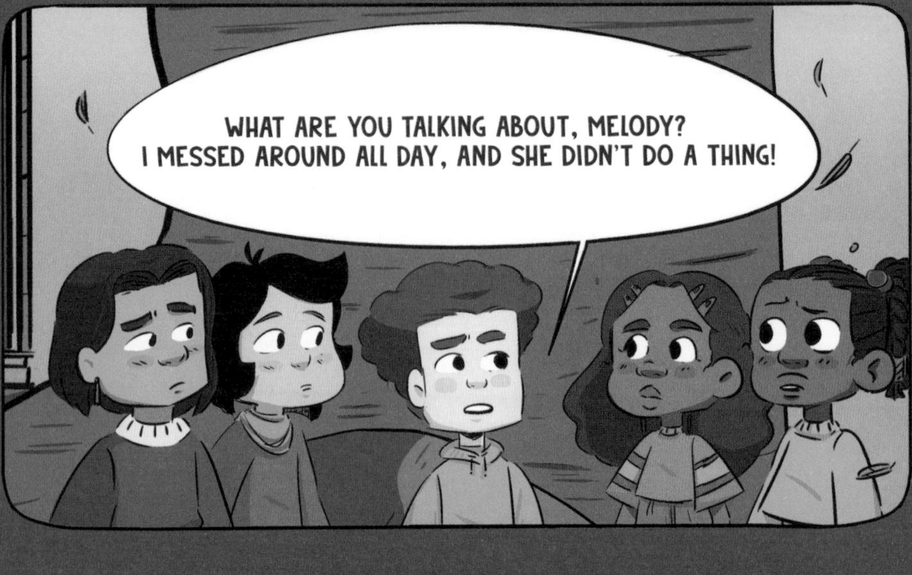
WHAT ARE YOU TALKING ABOUT, MELODY? I MESSED AROUND ALL DAY, AND SHE DIDN'T DO A THING!

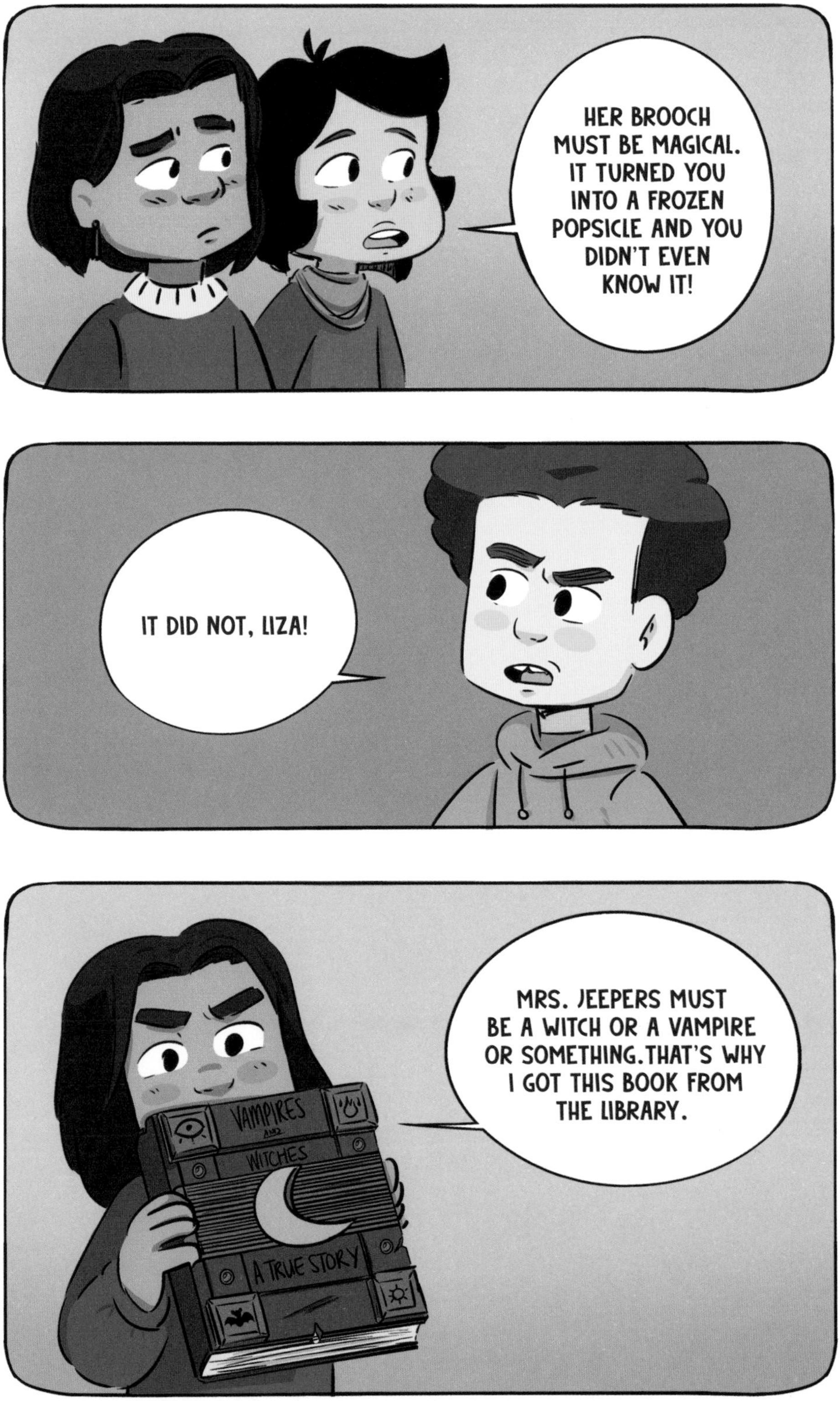
HER BROOCH MUST BE MAGICAL. IT TURNED YOU INTO A FROZEN POPSICLE AND YOU DIDN'T EVEN KNOW IT!
IT DID NOT, LIZA!
MRS. JEEPERS MUST BE A WITCH OR A VAMPIRE OR SOMETHING. THAT'S WHY I GOT THIS BOOK FROM THE LIBRARY.
VAMPIRES AND WITCHES
A TRUE STORY

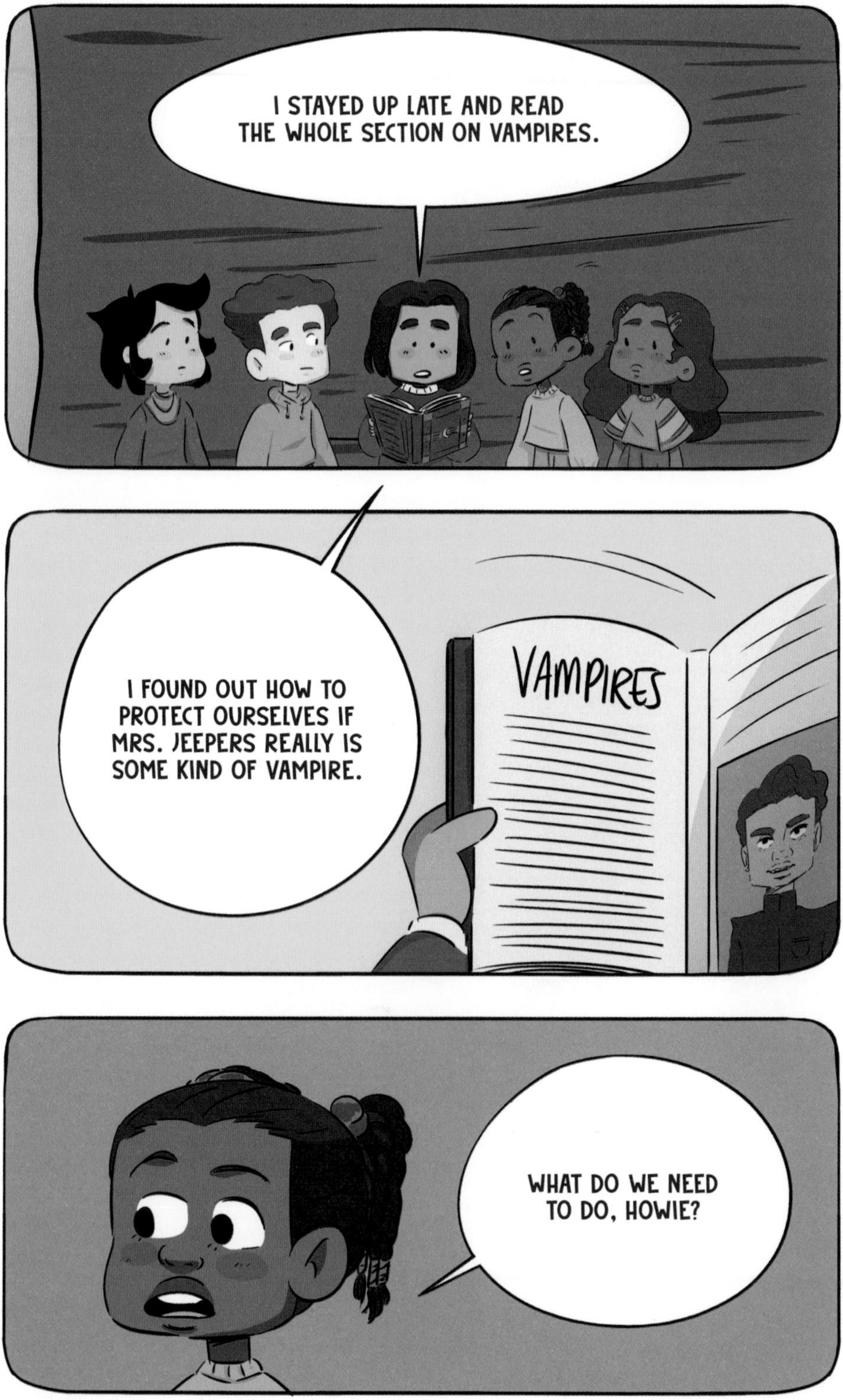
I STAYED UP LATE AND READ THE WHOLE SECTION ON VAMPIRES.
I FOUND OUT HOW TO PROTECT OURSELVES IF MRS. JEEPERS REALLY IS SOME KIND OF VAMPIRE.
VAMPIRES
WHAT DO WE NEED TO DO, HOWIE?

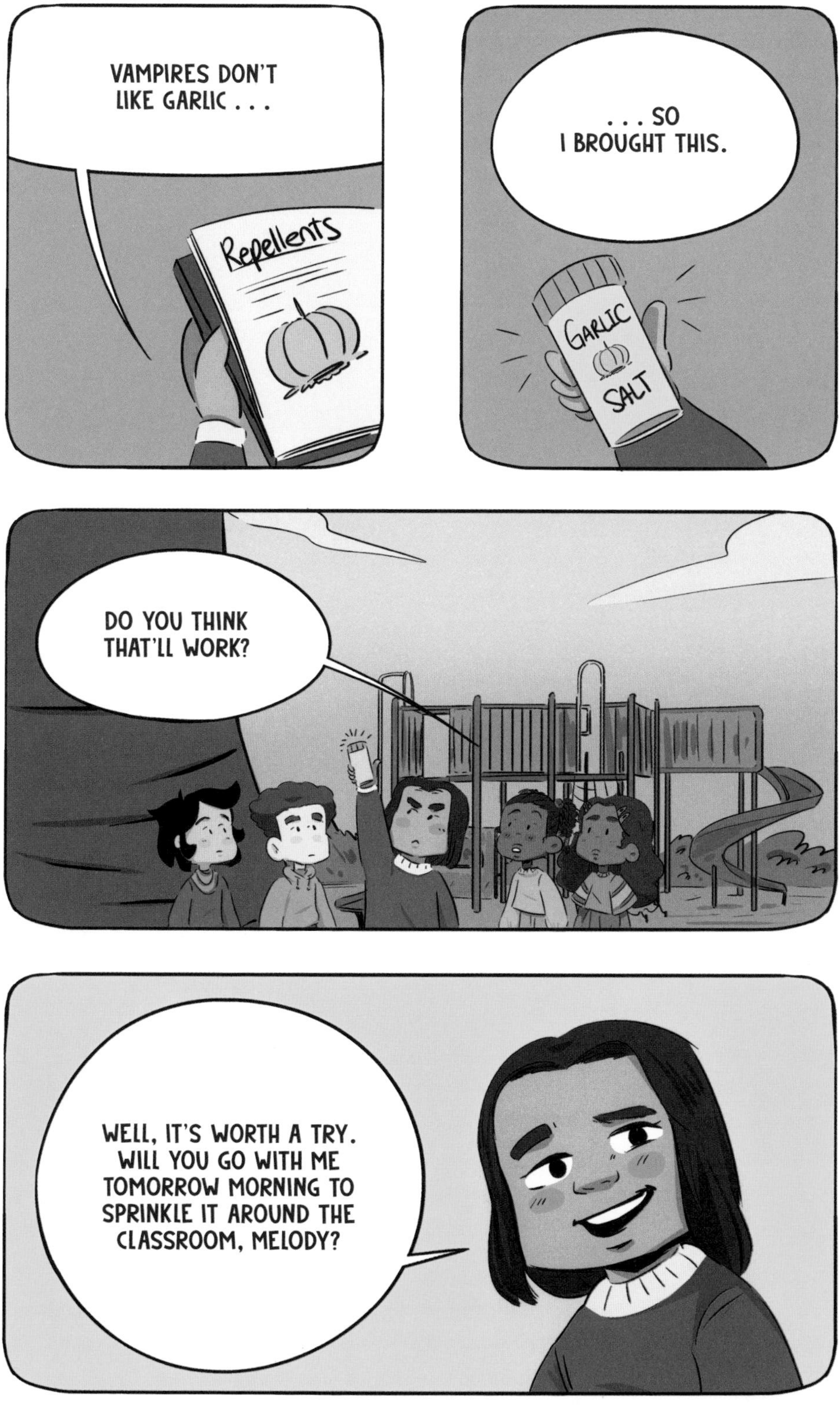
VAMPIRES DON'T LIKE GARLIC . . .
Repellents
. . . SO I BROUGHT THIS.
GARLIC SALT
DO YOU THINK THAT'LL WORK?
WELL, IT'S WORTH A TRY. WILL YOU GO WITH ME TOMORROW MORNING TO SPRINKLE IT AROUND THE CLASSROOM, MELODY?

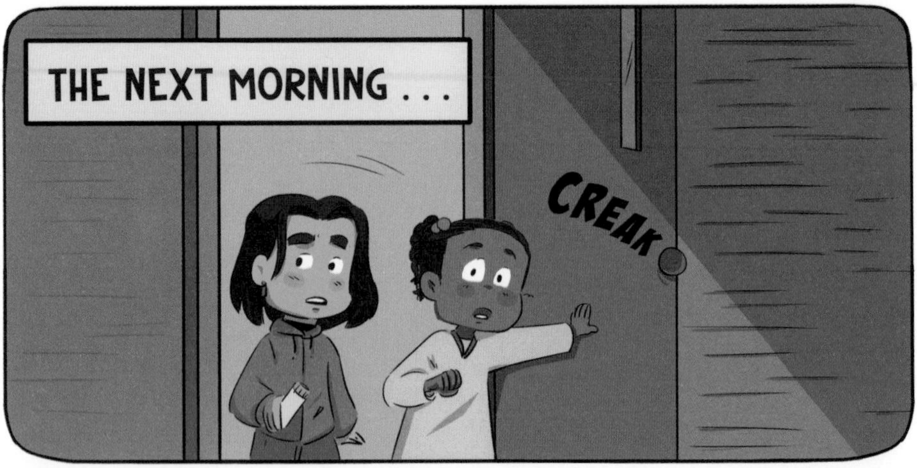
THE NEXT MORNING . . .
CREAK

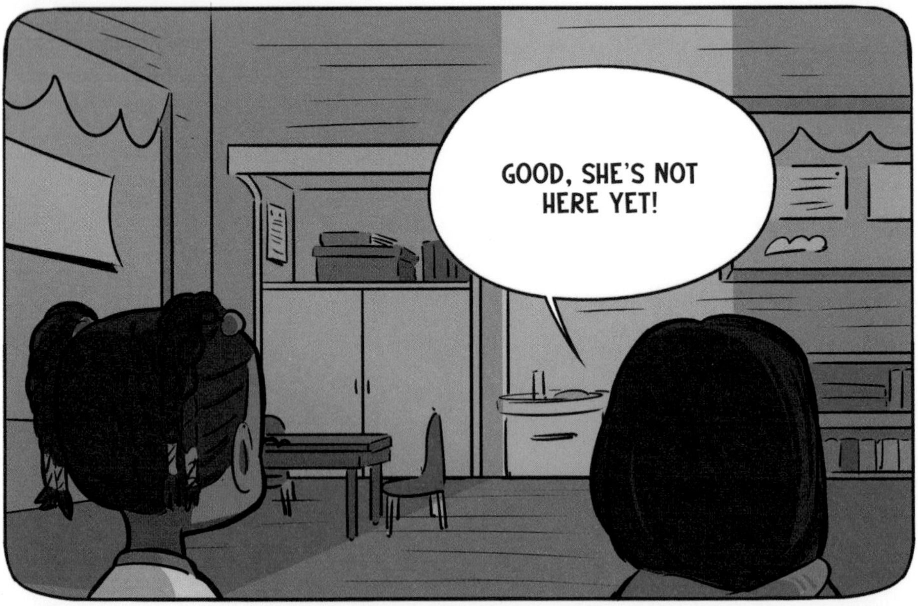
GOOD, SHE'S NOT HERE YET!

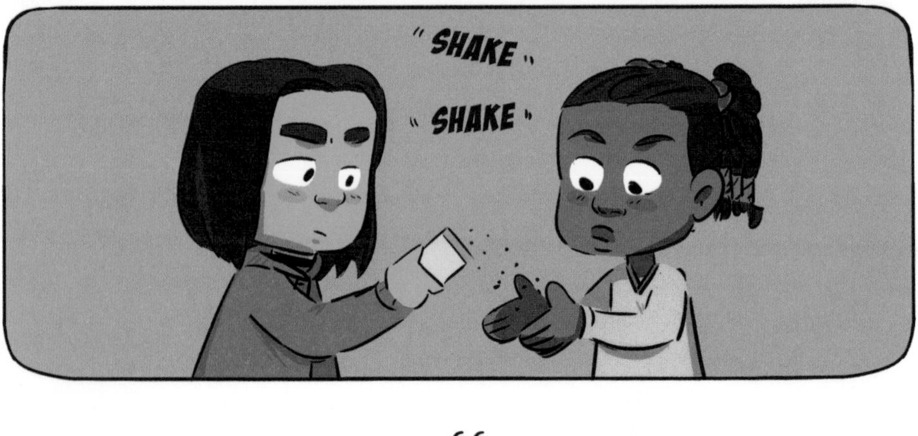
"SHAKE"
"SHAKE"

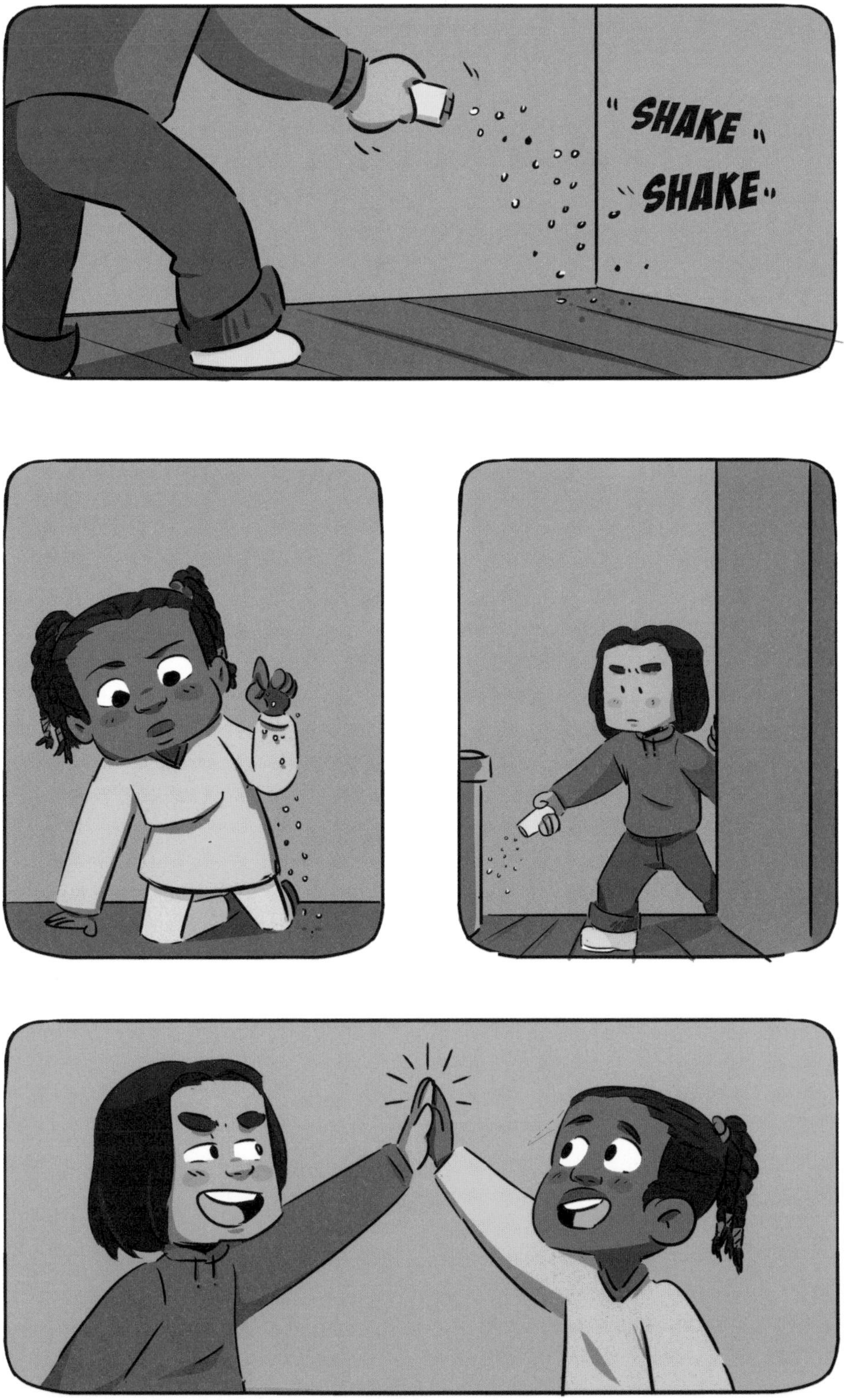
SHAKE
SHAKE

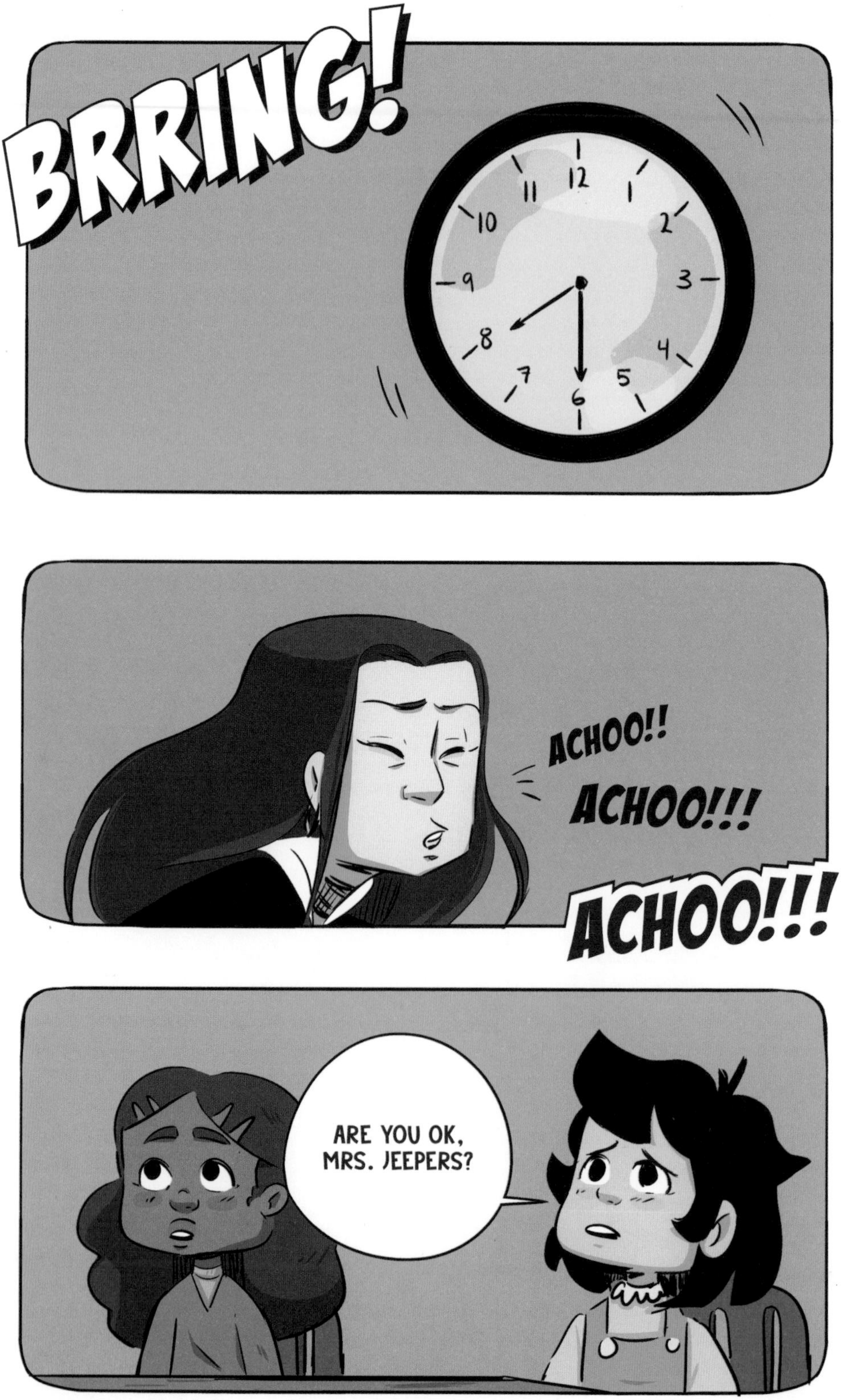
BRRING!
ACHOO!!
ACHOO!!!
ACHOO!!!
ARE YOU OK, MRS. JEEPERS?

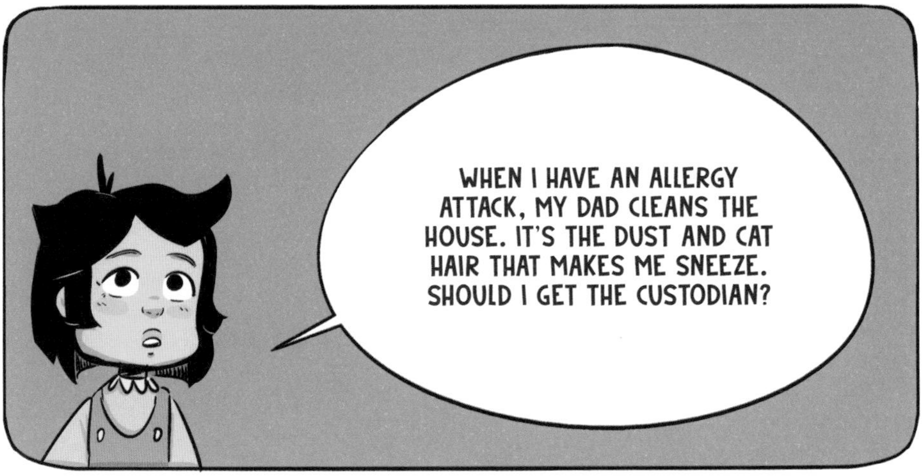
WHEN I HAVE AN ALLERGY ATTACK, MY DAD CLEANS THE HOUSE. IT'S THE DUST AND CAT HAIR THAT MAKES ME SNEEZE. SHOULD I GET THE CUSTODIAN?

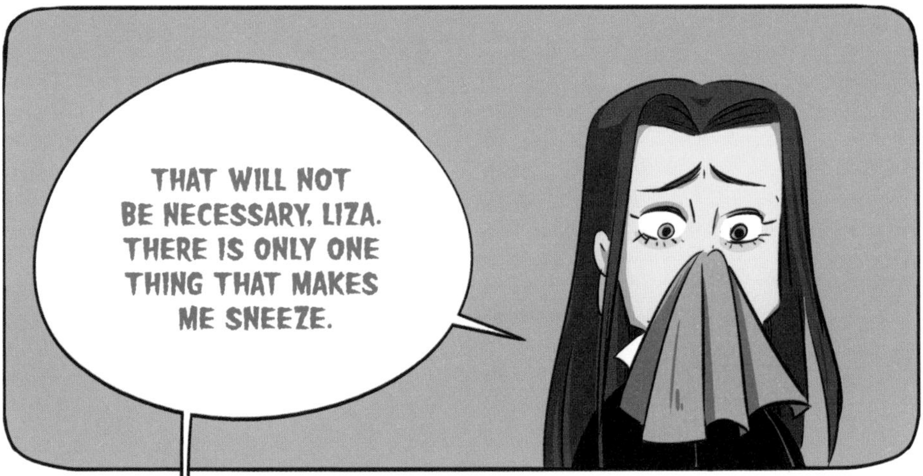
THAT WILL NOT BE NECESSARY, LIZA. THERE IS ONLY ONE THING THAT MAKES ME SNEEZE.

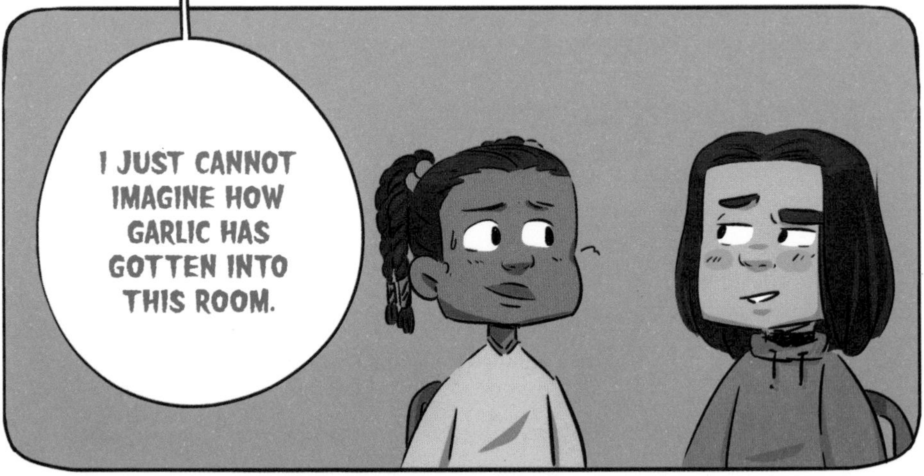
I JUST CANNOT IMAGINE HOW GARLIC HAS GOTTEN INTO THIS ROOM.

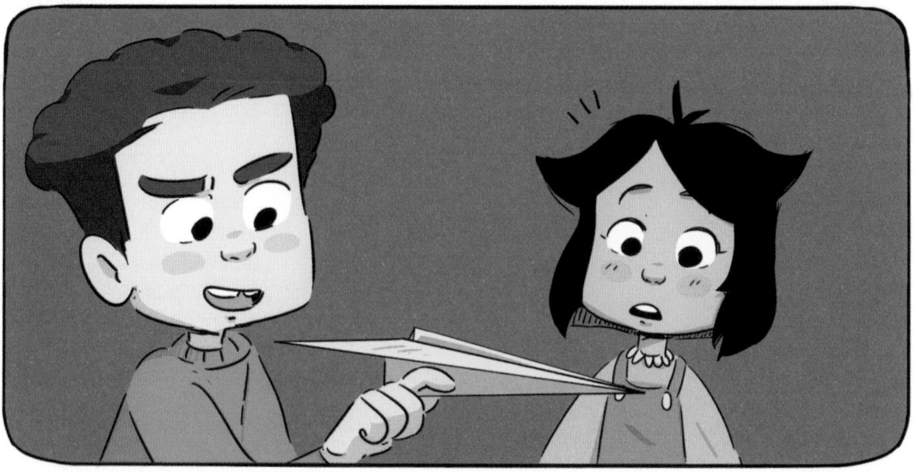

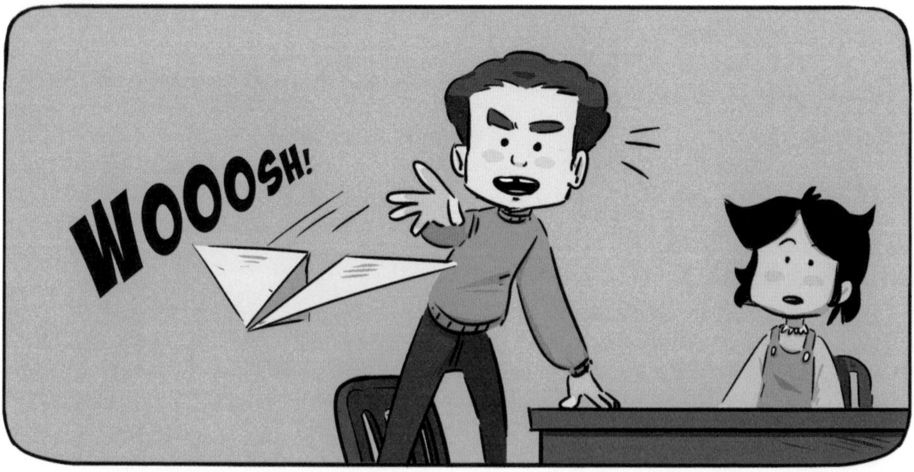
WOOOSH!

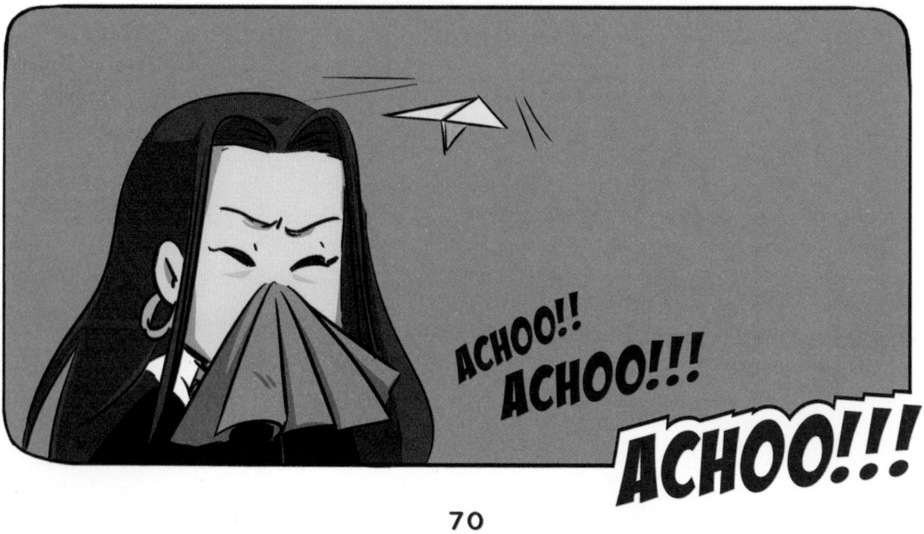
ACHOO!!
ACHOO!!!
ACHOO!!!

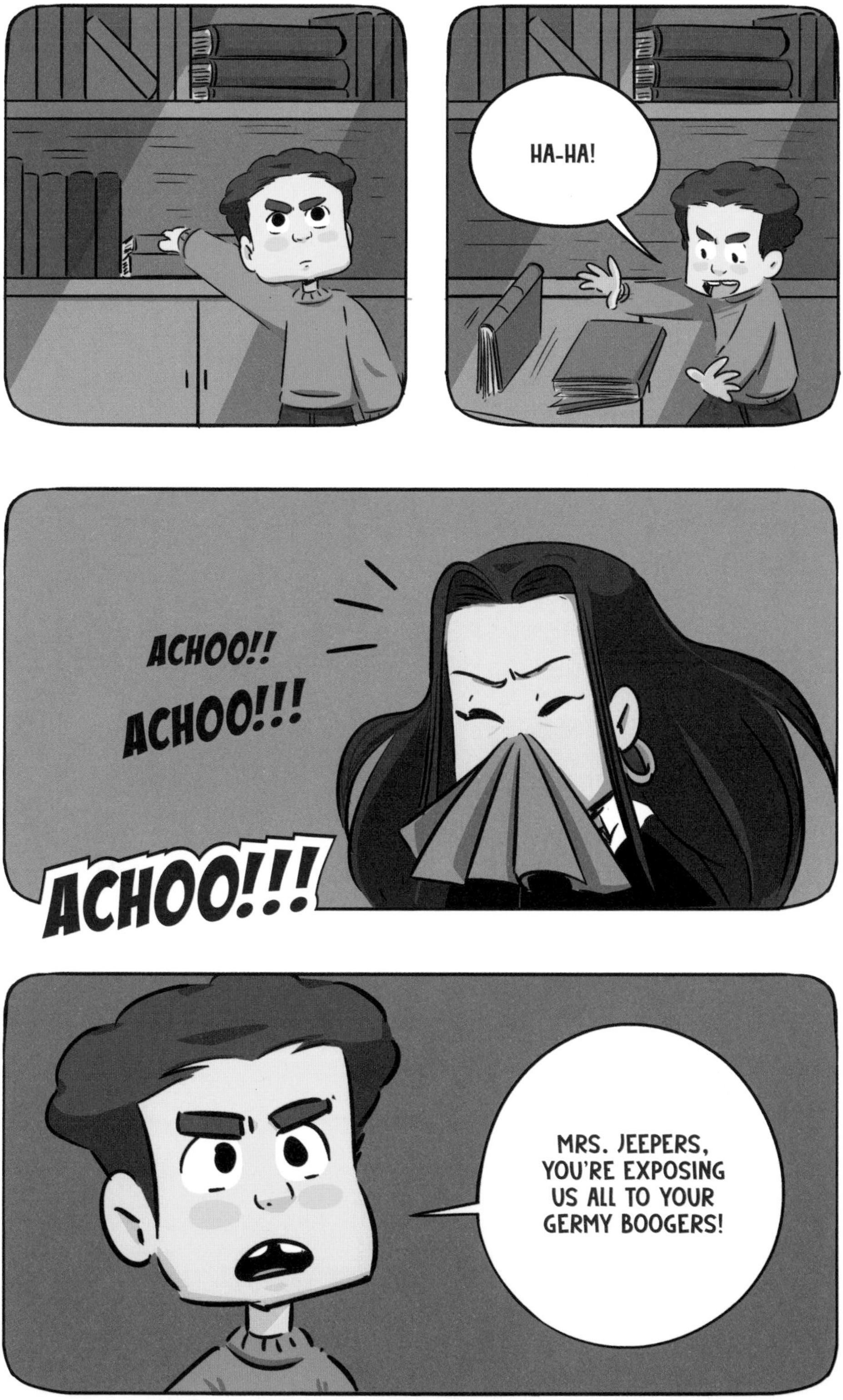
HA-HA!
ACHOO!!
ACHOO!!!
ACHOO!!!
MRS. JEEPERS, YOU'RE EXPOSING US ALL TO YOUR GERMY BOOGERS!

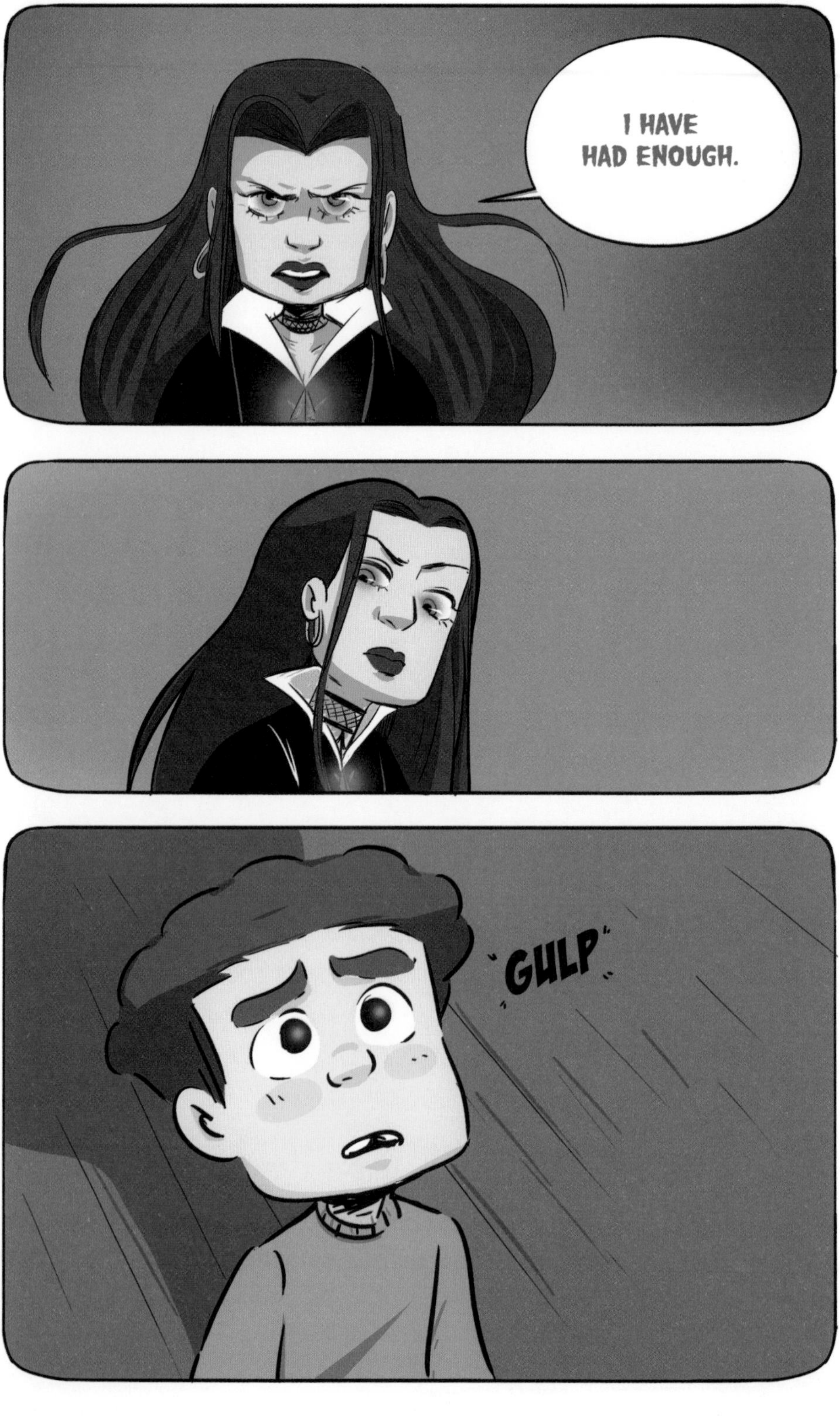
I HAVE HAD ENOUGH.
GULP

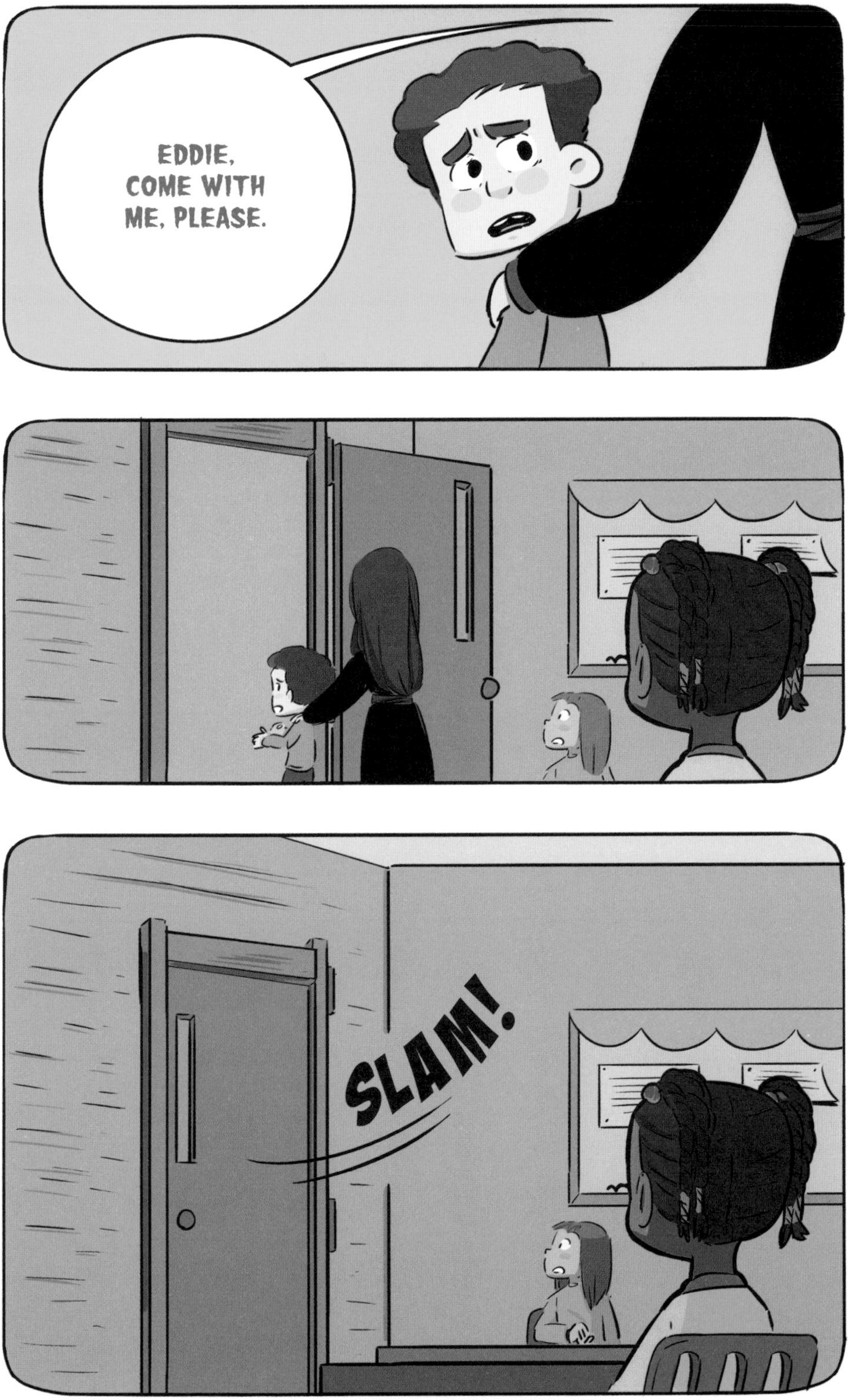
EDDIE, COME WITH ME, PLEASE.
SLAM!

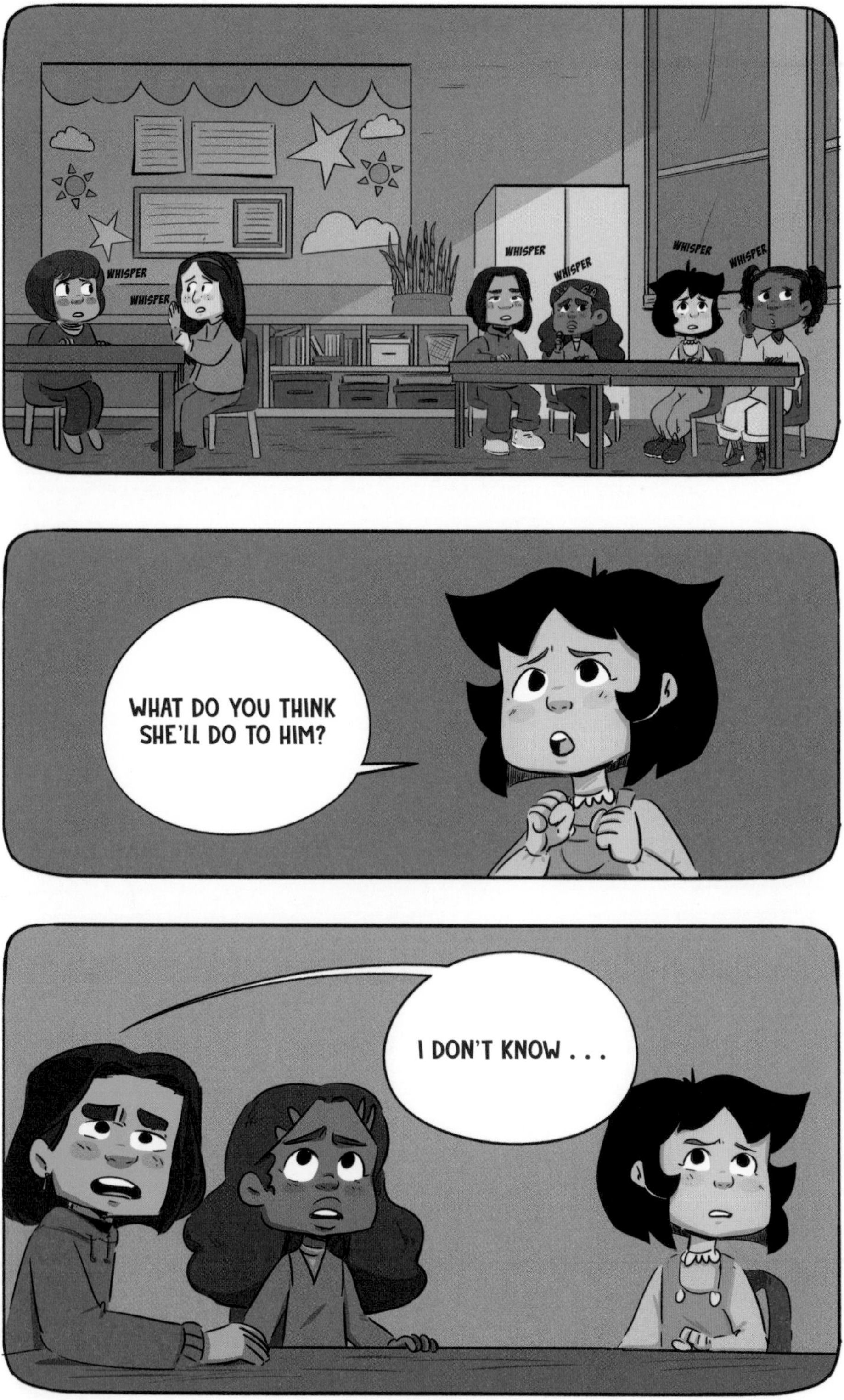
WHISPER
WHISPER
WHISPER
WHISPER
WHISPER
WHISPER
WHAT DO YOU THINK SHE'LL DO TO HIM?
I DON'T KNOW . . .

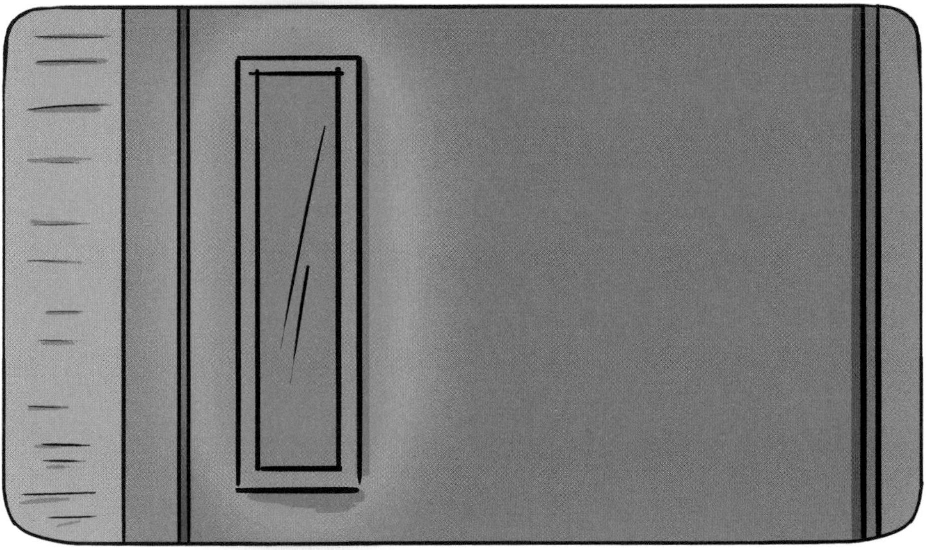

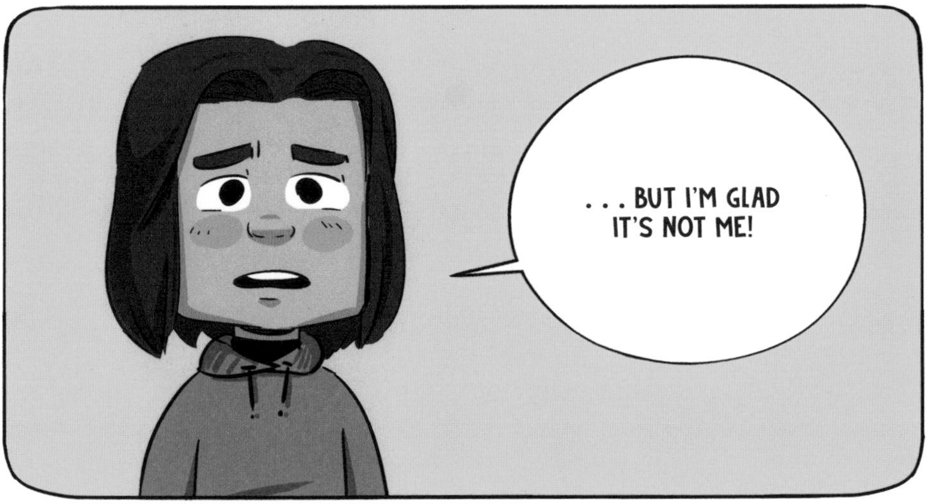
. . . BUT I'M GLAD IT'S NOT ME!

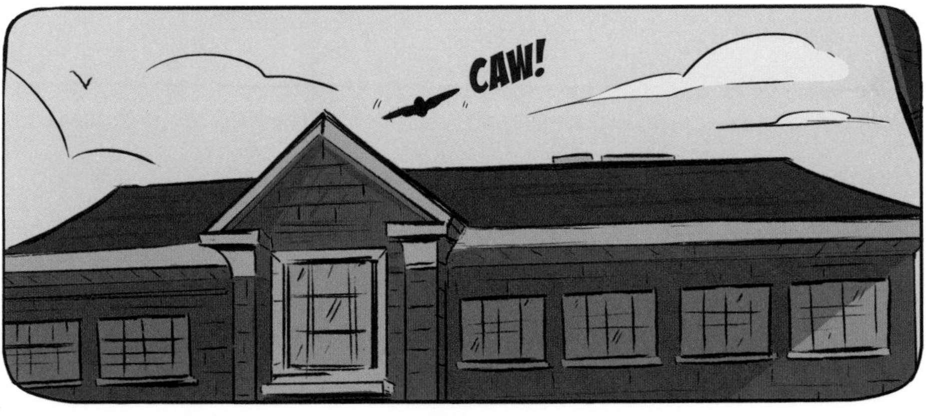
CAW!

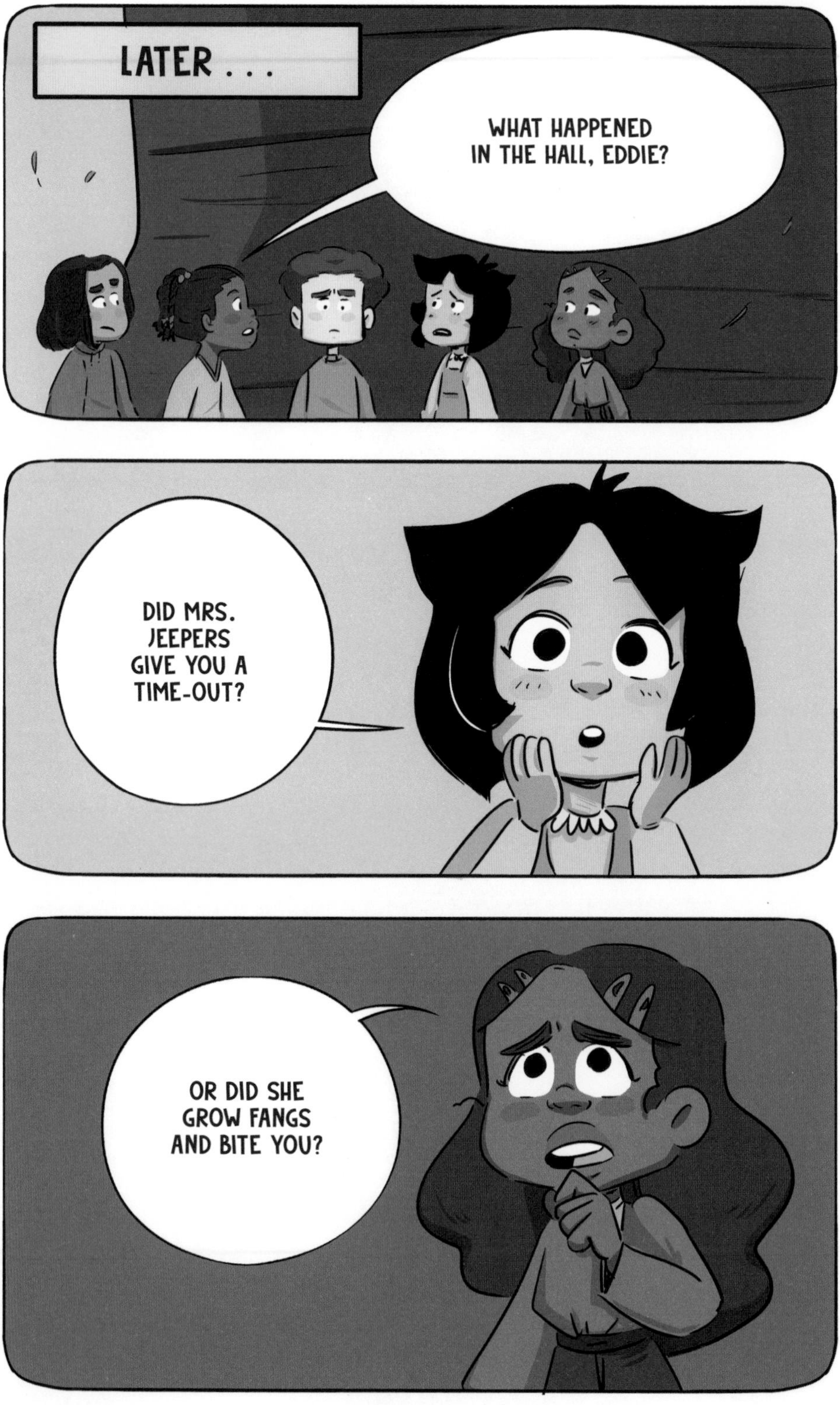
LATER . . .
WHAT HAPPENED IN THE HALL, EDDIE?
DID MRS. JEEPERS GIVE YOU A TIME-OUT?
OR DID SHE GROW FANGS AND BITE YOU?

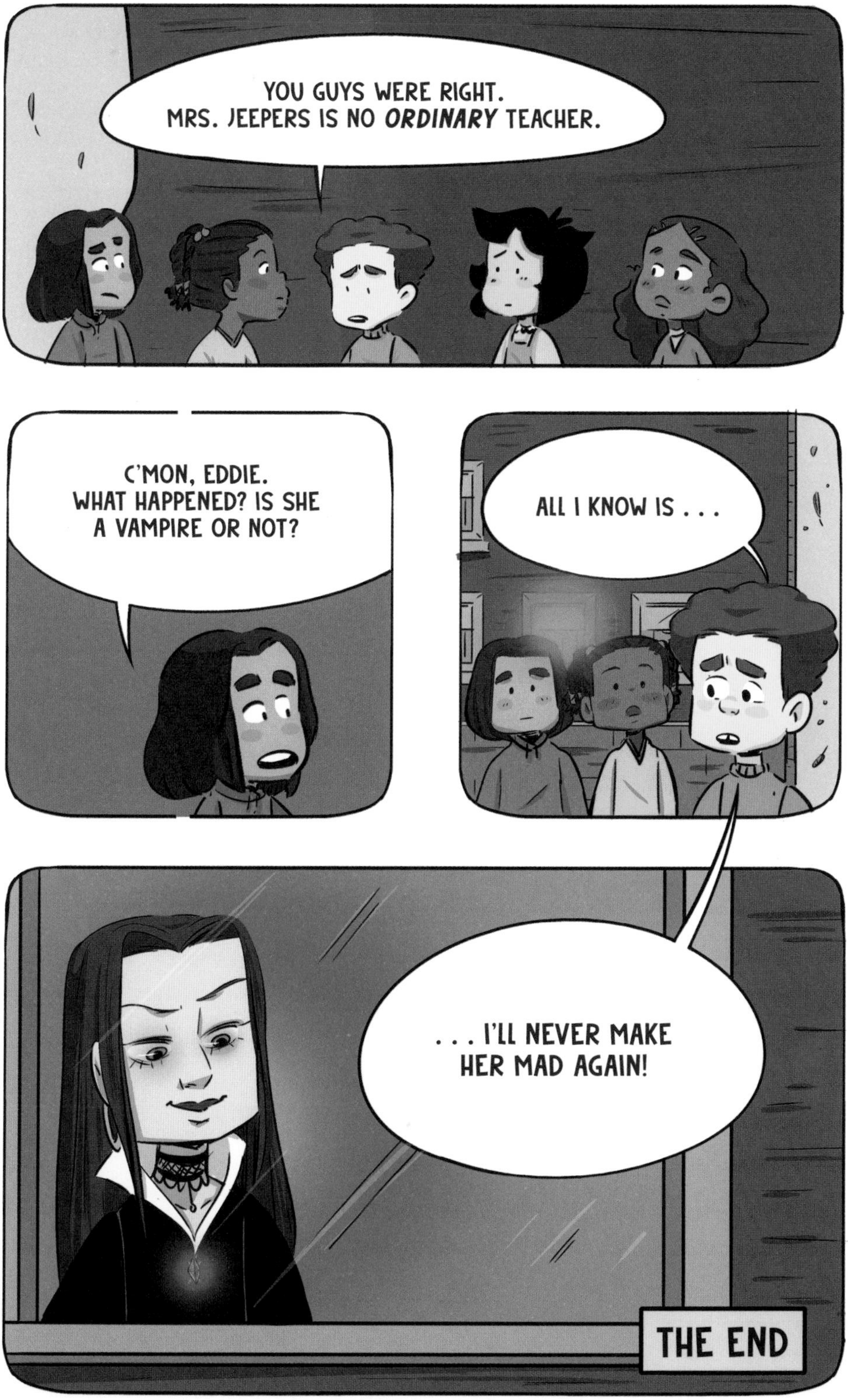
YOU GUYS WERE RIGHT. MRS. JEEPERS IS NO *ORDINARY* TEACHER.
C'MON, EDDIE. WHAT HAPPENED? IS SHE A VAMPIRE OR NOT?
ALL I KNOW IS . . .
. . . I'LL NEVER MAKE HER MAD AGAIN!
THE END

MARCIA THORNTON JONES is an award-winning author who has published 131 books for children, including the Adventures of the Bailey School Kids series, *Woodford Brave*, *Ratfink*, and *Champ*. Marcia lives with her husband, Steve, and two cats in Lexington, Kentucky, where she continues to write, mentor writers, and teach writing classes. She is the coordinator of the Carnegie Center Author Academy, an intensive one-on-one writing program for adult writers working toward publication.

DEBBIE DADEY grew up in Kentucky and now lives in a log cabin in Tennessee with her husband and a greyhound rescue. Her three adult children continue to inspire her. A former first grade teacher and school librarian, she is the author and coauthor of 179 books, including the Adventures of the Bailey School Kids series. Her newest series, Mermaid Tales, is a multicultural series from Simon and Schuster. She also coauthored *Writing for Kids: The Ultimate Guide* with Marcia Thornton Jones.

PEARL LOW is an Afro Asian artist based in Vancouver, Canada. Her works are rooted in themes of self-love, acceptance, and Chinese and Jamaican Canadian experiences. She works in comics and animation and won an Oscar in 2020 for her work on the short film *Hair Love*.